"I Do..."
How To...

Maudie told Keega[...]
curious—that is, I thought about— One hand
waved indecisively. "The thing is, I—"

"Wondered what it would be like to make love with
me," he finished for her when it seemed as if she
might expire before she could get it out.

"Sort of. Well, yes. I don't know exactly why—I
mean, I never think about that sort of thing
anymore. Very rarely. Almost never. I stay so busy,
what with my work and just surviving, that it doesn't
leave a whole lot of time for, umm . . . fantasizing."

Keegan squeezed her and reluctantly slid his leg off
hers, leaving her free to escape if she wanted to,
because he was just beginning to understand how
much her freedom really meant to her.

Dear Reader,

As the weather gets cold, cold, cold, Silhouette Desire gets hot, hot, hot! (If you live in Florida, Southern California or some other *warm* place, just imagine us living up north, *freezing!*) Anyway, here at Desire, we're generating *our* heat from six sensuous stories written by six spectacular authors. And they're all here, this month, in our HEAT UP YOUR WINTER collection.

Just take a look at this fabulous line-up: a *Man of the Month* from Lass Small; the next installment in the SOMETHING WILD series by Ann Major; and fantastic stories by Dixie Browning, Barbara Boswell, Mary Lynn Baxter and Robin Elliott. And I'm sure you've already noticed that this is one of our now-famous MONTHS OF MEN, with six sinfully sexy hero portraits on the front covers. (Aren't these guys *cute?*)

At Silhouette Desire we're dedicated to bringing you the very best short, sexy books around. Let us know—do you think we're succeeding? Are the books *too* sexy? Could you stand some more sizzle? Or maybe you think they're "just right." Write me! I'm here to listen.

In the meantime, HEAT UP YOUR WINTER with Silhouette Desire.

All the best,

Lucia Macro
Senior Editor

DIXIE
BROWNING
KEEGAN'S HUNT

SILHOUETTE *Desire®*

Published by Silhouette Books

America's Publisher of Contemporary Romance

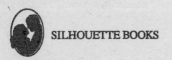

SILHOUETTE BOOKS

ISBN 0-373-05820-9

KEEGAN'S HUNT

Printed in U.S.A.

Books by Dixie Browning

DIXIE BROWNING

has written over fifty books for Silhouette since 1980. She is a charter member of the Romance Writers of America and an award-winning author and has toured extensively for Silhouette Books. She also writes historical romances with her sister under the name Bronwyn Williams.

For the wonderful man who's responsible for
Hawk's Nest, Heron's Rest and Rabbit Gum—
Lou Browning

Prologue

"**I** can't *stand* it! You've got to *do* something!"

"You mean, like—get rid of him?"

"I mean, like whatever it takes! Yesterday, he made Benji polish his track shoes. Can you believe it?"

"Ah, Babe, that's no big deal. Takes a while to get over the spit and polish syndrome, I guess."

"And he's spoiling them rotten, too. He spends more time with the kids than he does with anyone else, and they all think he's Santa Claus and the Easter Bunny wrapped up in one, even when he makes them toe the line. Honestly, Ken, it's not fair!"

"Honey, he's an uncle, not a parent. Uncles have special privileges—sort of like grandparents, I guess. At least they're staying out of trouble. For Edie's pair, that's saying a lot."

"That's another thing. Edie says he's promised to clean up her backyard. Do you know how many years it's taken her to achieve that natural effect? Do you have any idea how much damage your sainted brother can do in five minutes when he gets on one of his neatness kicks? Heaven help me, I almost wish—''

''No, you don't. Don't even think it.''

''Oh, I know, I know—I love him, too, and I wore my knees out praying every minute he was being held prisoner over in that awful place. But honestly, Ken, he's driving me nuts!''

''He's driving us all nuts. But, Babe, you have to understand, that's just Rich's way. I mean, you have to remember, he had all us kids to boss around after Dad died, with Mother being sick so much. Heck, he was probably putting half the Air Force Academy through their paces before he'd been there six weeks. Mother use to say he was just like Dad—I don't remember. But he doesn't mean anything by it, it's just his nature. If it hadn't been for—''

''I know, if it hadn't been for this awful war thing, and if he hadn't been sent over there to fly those noisy monsters of his, and—''

''F-15s.''

''Whatever. And I'm proud of him, Kenny, I really am, but honest to God, the next time he tries to organize my shopping list according to the layout of the market floorplan, I'm going to crown him on his everloving cowlick. All three of 'em!''

''Just so you don't hurt his back.''

''Oh, I know, I know, I'm an unnatural sister-in-law. And he is a war hero, and an injured POW and all, only...''

''Right. Hey, Babe? You don't suppose Alice wants him back, do you? Maybe if we could get those two together again...''

"Over my dead body. He may be driving us all up the wall, but he's still my favorite brother-in-law, and underneath all that cast-iron hup, two, three, four junk, he's still an old sweetie pie. Besides, Alice is a slut. I know for a fact she was having an affair with that guy in accounts collectable before she and Rich had even been married a year."

"Yeah, well . . . maybe not Alice again, then, but Rich is only forty-two. I doubt if he's quite over the hill yet."

"Believe me, love, your big brother is far from over the hill. There are some things even a happily married and much harried sister-in-law can tell at a glance, and Rich Keegan, whatever other problems he may have, is most definitely not over any hill."

"Hey, watch it, there! Don't go getting too enthusiastic. Seriously, though, I've been thinking, Babe. You remember me telling you about this old hunt club place Grandpop Keegan used to have somewhere down in the Carolinas? North, I think it was. Out on some island?"

"Was it part of the estate? I missed most of the will stuff. Stevie was potty training then, remember? I had to take him out, and when I got back, you guys had already reached the cake and sherry stage."

"There was something about this ninety-nine year lease that's scheduled to expire this coming March. Hornstein didn't know much more than that. He just came across the lease agreement in that box of old papers I dug up in Grandpop's things and figured since it only had a few months to run, there wasn't much point in digging into it. Anyway, as far as we know, nobody in our generation's ever seen the place. I doubt if it's even still standing."

"So why bring it up? Is it going to cure Benji's bronchitis or pay Bitsy's tuition at Country Day School?"

"No, but it just might cure something else that's been driving us all nuts for the past few months."

"You mean—?"

"Exactly. What my big bossy brother needs is a project."

"Boy, does he ever!"

"So why not—?"

"Yeah ... why not?"

CHAPTER ONE

One

Maudie bent over from the waist and squinted at the tracks in the damp sand. They were big, about a men's size eleven, she judged, placing her own women's size five in the clearest one. From the depth in the soft sand, she'd put him at either seven feet tall and skinny as a bed slat, or five feet nothing and round as a pumpkin. Or some combination of the two, which wasn't a lot to go on.

She followed the trail to the edge of the woods and lost it in the pine straw. What now? Check out the cottages first? They'd be the most likely target for a thief. On the other hand, she had two six-volt batteries and a spare outboard in the boat house.

Oh, drat! If she hadn't taken the shortcut back after her morning rounds, she would've caught him red-handed.

At least it was a "him" and not a "them," which meant that the odds were more or less even. Probably some bored tourist who was either illiterate or who thought he was above the law.

Making up her mind abruptly, she veered down toward the beach. Earlier she'd thought she heard an outboard, but she hadn't paid much attention. This was boat country. In the summertime, there were crabbers, clammers and sportfishermen swarming all over the place. She grew so used to hearing boat motors, she hardly even noticed them.

But this was January. Too early for crabbers and clammers, and nobody fished commercially around Coronoke Island. Too many snags. Bit by bit, the island had washed away over the years, first the old bridge that used to go to Hatteras, and then the ferry landing, and even some of the cottages that used to stand on stilts out over the water. But now that the place was well and truly off the beaten track, every two-bit Columbus with a rowboat seemed determined to rediscover it.

Silently tapping her foot in the sand, Maudie muttered under her breath. It wasn't enough that a branch had blown down and broken a section of gutter on Hawk's Nest, or that that blasted racoon had torn another hole in the screen at Heron's Rest after she'd just mended it last week. Or that one of the shutter hinges had rusted off on Blackbeard's and she'd have to go locate a replacement. She had more to do today than go traipsing all over the island tracking down some idiot trespasser who thought Private Property and Keep Out signs were meant for ordinary mortals.

Bloody tourists! The season used to end in November except for a handful of windsurfers and a few diehard fishermen, after which all the locals could relax and settle down for a brief, peaceful winter. Now just let the sun shine for three days in succession, any month of the year, and tourists sprouted like fungus after a five day rain.

Maudie was a conscientious woman. It was one of the reasons, other than family connections, she had landed this job in the first place, the other reason being that no one else wanted it. Cottage maintenance crews were hard to keep, even over on Hatteras. Toss a twenty-minute boat ride into the equation and it was a seller's market. The real estate broker who managed the five Coronoke cottages had practically gone down on his knees when he'd heard she would even consider taking on the job.

A few minutes later, Maudie came out of the woods in the clearing overlooking the small, two-plank pier. That, too, was her responsibility, along with the privately owned cottages and the dilapidated old hunt club where she had set up housekeeping eighteen months ago after her daughter had gone off to college.

Just as she'd thought, there was a strange boat tied up beside her own flat-bottomed skiff. A battered aluminum job that she recognized as a rental, only this one had twice the necessary horsepower, which usually indicated a rooster tail artist. 9.9 was standard. 25 was absurd.

"Oh, great," she muttered. "Just what I need to make my day complete, a run-in with some macho power freak with a hot-rod boat and a few hours to kill!"

In cases such as this, it was safer to call in reinforcements. Green eyes flashing, Maudie reversed her course, taking the shortcut through the woods. Trespassers, she had learned, came in different degrees of unwelcome. Family groups were one thing. Bird watchers and turtle huggers she could handle.

Seagoing hot-rodders fueled with a mixture of beer and testosterone were another thing entirely. Maudie had her own way of dealing with them. A woman living alone on an island learned very quickly.

But then, when it came to men, Maudie's education had begun a long time ago. About twenty years ago, to be exact.

In no time at all she was back in the live oak grove overlooking the pier, her .410 cradled in her arm and a grim look on her face. Her door had been left ajar. She always closed it when she left, to keep the local livestock from moving inside. No one had ever broken in before, probably because they couldn't imagine anyone's living in such a tumbledown ruin.

Which was precisely what she wanted them to think. A low profile was an excellent defense.

Now some stinking lowlife had broken into her home! Right into her front room! Thank God she had locked the rest of the house, from habit more than anything else. The front room didn't have a lock. To be truthful, it hardly even had a door—only a makeshift one she had pieced together and hung herself.

That creep! Taking care not to attract attention, Maudie scanned the woods and then the beach. Nothing moved. Not even a fish crow. Which meant he was probably checking out the cottages on the other side of the island to see what he could steal. If she weren't afraid he would get away, she would double back to the Hunt and radio the sheriff over on Hatteras. Or maybe she would just lop off his head and plunk it on the bowsprit of her skiff à la Blackbeard.

Nope...too messy. Besides, she didn't have a bowsprit. Or even a lopper.

And then she noticed the three boxes and the stack of paintings—*her paintings!*—propped up against the boat house.

Eyes narrowed against the glare of the midday sun, Maudie propped her shotgun against a tree and ran swiftly down to the pier. Ignoring the stacked canvases, she hurried to the rented boat tied up beside her own skiff.

It took only a moment to remove the wire to the spark plug. Tucking it into her pocket along with two tissues, a roasted peanut and a copper nail, she hurried back up to the woods to wait. We'd see how far he'd get without his twenty-five horses.

Fuming, Maudie picked up the heavy shotgun and settled down to wait. Darn it, she hadn't painted all those lighthouses, sand dunes and fishing boats to satisfy her inner muse. That was her entire winter's output! Her salary as caretaker, maintenance woman and cleaning crew to Coronoke's five cottages bought her groceries, paid her taxes and took care of the never-ending expense of having a daughter in college, over and above what Sanford's trust provided. The painting money was her nest egg, for when Ann Mary graduated and the two of them found a place on the mainland.

She heard him even before she saw him. He was making no effort to be quiet. In fact, the thieving jerk was whistling!

For a single moment, Maudie Winters almost wished she had a shell in the single chamber of her ancient .410 gauge shotgun.

Rich—Richmond Keegan to his friends—wondered how the devil the old man could have forgotten all this stuff. Some of it looked almost new. The place had been built by Rich's great-grandfather, and used by his grandfather and maybe even his father. Rich didn't remember much about the man who had survived two wars only to be brought down by a ruptured appendix, leaving behind seven kids and an invalid widow.

The old place looked about ready to collapse at any moment. There'd been a door at the other end of the room, but it had evidently been jammed and he hadn't dared exert any real force. Without venturing beyond the first room, he'd retrieved what he could easily carry, not that any of it looked to be valuable. Still, the kids might like having a small piece of Keegan history, such as it was.

Careful to use his knees instead of his back, Rich lowered another box of books and two more paintings. Then he removed a pair of ruby red glasses from his pockets. The glasses, still sitting on a table as if they'd been used only yesterday, had caught his eye and he'd brought them along. Ken's wife might like them. Or one of his sisters. They were probably dime store stuff, but they were kind of pretty. For all he knew, the books might be junk, too. Probably too far gone with damp rot and mildew to be much good to anyone. Still, it would be interesting to glance through the titles when he had time and discover what previous generations of Keegans had considered worth reading.

The paintings had come as a surprise. Rich didn't know a damned thing about art. Hadn't even known the old man had collected the stuff. Still, it seemed a shame just to leave it all behind to rot or be ripped off or washed away by the next hurricane.

Pity about the old place. It must have been impressive in his great-grandfather's day. It was too far gone to be worth restoring, though, especially considering that whatever claim his family might once have had on the property would end in a few months' time.

There was a fresh wind blowing in his face, and he stood there for a moment, gazing out across the Pamlico Sound to where Hatteras lay, a long, hazy blip on the horizon. Inhaling deeply, he felt oddly invigorated by the mixture of salt, pine resin and something else—something damp and primal and fecund.

Probably a muddy marsh, he told himself, turning away. Keegan wasn't a poetic type. Pragmatic by nature, he had never had time to waste on flights of fancy. Still, he couldn't help but wonder when the last Keegan had visited this place. So much had happened over the past forty-odd years. Wars—not to mention all the military interventions and peacekeeping actions. Marriages—there'd been seven of those in the immediate family, including his own. Births. He had more nieces and nephews than he could keep up with. Deaths. His parents. His grandparents. Ken and Babe's infant son. An uncle who had been killed in Nam, who had been only a few years older than Rich himself.

And divorces, he reminded himself. Again, including his own.

Keegan's Hunt, he mused, caught up in an uncharacteristic mood of nostalgia. Funny how a man could spend his entire life building an empire, and in the end, it came down to this. A few boxes of mildewed books and a few seascapes that no one had even bothered to frame.

Of course, there did happen to be one small town in northern Connecticut where just about every family was related to, if not actually a descendant of, the original Keegan who had come over in steerage to escape the great potato famine. If things had turned out differently, Rich might have left behind a living memento of his own existence, but it hadn't been in the cards. Rather than waste time regretting it, he had decided to enjoy taking a hand in the raising of his nieces and nephews.

Rubbing the small of his back, he stood and gazed down at the cartons, some of which were damned heavy. Starting tomorrow he had a long, tiresome drive ahead of him.

But first there was the loading, unloading and then re-loading the stuff from boat to car. He'd better dig out his brace. In deference to his back, he had taken the drive south in easy stages. At this rate, he might not make it home until spring.

Keegan was carefully lifting the first carton of books, preparing to step down into his rented boat, when a soft, husky voice spoke from somewhere behind him. "Hold it right there, mister."

He froze. The short hair on the back of his neck stood up. "No problem," he said, wondering who the hell had got the drop on him, and why. Wondering just when he had lost his edge. It wasn't like him to drop his guard, even now that danger was a thing of the past.

"Put 'em down very carefully. Watch it! Don't knock that canvas over! Carefully, I said!"

A woman.

A woman? "Easy, lady, I'm not looking for trouble."

"Too late. You've already found it. Now, turn around. Slowly. Keep your hands away from your body, this thing's loaded with double-ought buckshot, and the barrel's got a choke on it you wouldn't believe."

Systems check: low on fuel. Unarmed. Uncharted territory.

Unidentified enemy closing fast.

Priority check: disarm enemy. Get the hell out.

Keegan took his time. Captivity, hospitalization, and the frustration of being out of the service after twenty-two years had honed his nerves to a fine edge. His body, except for a back that was still inclined to be temperamental, was in good fighting trim.

But a *woman?* A woman with a *shotgun?*

He turned slowly, his mind processing information almost faster than his eyes could feed it to his brain. She was small. No bigger than his eleven-year-old niece, but ballasted differently. A hell of a lot differently! Even before he spoke, his body began assimilating information on its own. And reacting.

"You want to tell me what your problem is?" he asked, his voice carefully devoid of all expression.

"You can't read, right?"

"Read?" His eyes narrowed on her face. With her back to the sun, she had the advantage, even without the gun.

"Signs. Like the one on the end of the pier that says Private Property? And the ones all over the island that say No Trespassing, and Keep Out, and Intruders Will Be Shot On Sight?"

"You made up that last one, right?"

The gun barrel came up a fraction until it was pointed at his chest instead of his groin. Which made him feel some better, but not a whole lot. "Anyone ever tell you it's not polite to point a loaded gun at an unarmed man?"

"Anyone ever tell you that No Trespassing means exactly that?"

Keegan blew a stream of air up over his suddenly damp face. He reminded himself that he'd been in far tighter situations and survived. But then, he'd always known the odds going in. This time he was operating at a disadvantage. Number one: he hadn't even known there were any odds. Number two: the little gun-toting mama—never mind that she was short-legged, broad-beamed and a tad too busty for a bona fide leg man—was just about the most provocative female he'd seen in a long, long time. Fragile, soft-spoken and defensive, she was the kind of woman that always brought out his protective instincts. Which, under the circumstances, was pretty damned bizarre.

She also brought out another kind of instinct, which, under the circumstances, was even more bizarre. Nice to

know he still had a few systems operating at peak effi-
ciency, he thought with a wry inward smile.

"I'm tempted to make you tote every bit of that stuff
back up to the house," the woman threatened. "If I didn't
want you out of my sight so much, I would."

"You're the boss. I was just retrieving a few family mementos for the next generation, but I can—"

"Family mementos! What are you, a long lost cousin or
something?"

Keegan shrugged off the remark. He had a more immediate worry. "Look, could you just lower that gun,
please?"

She dropped the barrel two inches and he summoned the
last of his fast dwindling patience. "Miss, I think there's
been some kind of a misunderstanding. You obviously—"

"You're right. There has been a misunderstanding. You
misunderstood the fact that those signs mean exactly what
they say."

Keegan had fought a lifelong battle with his hair-trigger
temper. He was in no mood to fight now. He was tired,
dammit. And she was being deliberately obstructive!

Ignoring the piece of antique artillery that was aimed
once more at his crotch, as if it were too heavy for her
small hands to support, he began stalking up the sloping
beach, his eyes, narrowed against the glaring sun, never
once leaving her face. The trouble was, other than the
damned shotgun in her hands, she was a real looker, from
the windblown snarl of silky brown hair to the shallow
cleft in her stubborn little chin. At the moment, however,
he was in no mood to be turned on by any mouthy little
female in tight jeans.

"Look, lady, I don't know who you are," he said, having approached to within a few feet of his quarry—so close

he could see the texture of her golden skin, so close he could catch a drift of something that smelled almost like clover overlaying the ambient scent of cedar, pine and salt marsh. "Look, we both know you're not going to shoot me, so why don't you put that thing down and tell me who you are, and who you think I am? There's obviously been a foul-up in communications."

"There's no foul-up. I know who I am. I don't give a—"

"Tsk-tsk—manners," Keegan taunted. Holding her eyes, which he saw for the first time were a dark green with lighter flecks, surrounded by thick, sun-tipped lashes, he slowly reached out a hand, intent on shifting the barrel of the gun off target.

He was tired. She was quick. Just as he grabbed hold of the gun barrel she jumped back, jerking him off balance. He didn't actually fall, but when the shaft of pain stabbed though his lower back, he sank to his knees with a groan that was wrenched all the way up from his gut.

"I didn't lay a hand on you! Quit that!" the woman cried.

Keegan could only shake his head. Oh, hell. Five days of driving. Four nights of motel mattresses. He had survived all that only to be brought down by a pint-size Venus with a shotgun that probably wouldn't have fired if she'd packed the barrel with nitro.

Maudie was scared. Was he playing some weird kind of game with her? She'd never seen a man react this way. On the rare occasions when a few words of advice hadn't been enough, the sight of her shotgun had always sent them on their way. One thing she'd learned early on was that men instinctively distrusted an armed woman. Knowing it, she deliberately used their fear against them. It had always

worked before. At least none of them had ever turned
white, broken into a sweat and started groaning.

"Back," he muttered, and dutifully, she backed up a
few steps, still wary of a trick.

"Come here, dammit—help me lie down!" He was still
kneeling, his position awkward on the sloping beach.

"Keep your distance, mister. I wasn't born yesterday."

"Ah—" He uttered a four letter word that she'd been
spanked for using when she was four and a half. "Look,
I'm hardly in any condition to threaten your virtue,
sweetheart, so would you please just lighten up and put
down that thunder stick?"

Lowering the gun, but not releasing it, Maudie edged
closer. He really did look awful. Looked as if he were in
pain, in fact. His skin, which had appeared healthy enough
only a moment ago, was now fish-belly pale. And damp.
The eyes that only a moment before had looked like shards
of October sky had darkened with pain.

"You're hurting?" she ventured.

"You noticed," he said, the sarcasm not lessened by the
strained quality of his voice.

"Is it your heart?"

"No, dammit, it's my back! When you threw me off
balance—"

"When you tried to take my gun away from me, you
mean."

Rich closed his eyes. "Right. Look, I need to lie down
somewhere flat. This angle is killing me."

"Do you want me to go for a doctor? There's one over
on Hatteras, if he hasn't gone up the Banks."

"I don't need a doctor, I need a hard bed. Or a floor.
Anything, so long as I can lie flat for a few hours."

"What about medicine?"

"It's in my bag, in my car, over at the marina." If he'd known the place was booby-trapped, he'd have brought along a whole damned medevac unit as backup!

"If you think you can make it, I'll help you up to my place," she said warily. "You can rest there until you feel like leaving."

Until he felt like leaving? How about making that retroactive about six months? Six months ago he'd been feeling great, back in the bosom of his family after the nightmare of captivity, followed by a grueling tour of duty in an army hospital.

Or even six weeks. Six weeks ago he had just started seeing a woman. Nothing physical yet, but he'd had hopes in that direction. After Alice, he had planned to take it slow and easy. No involvement, no commitment. Just a nice, safe, companionable affair with a little sex thrown in for good measure once he was back in shape for it.

"Lady, you're going to have to put that overgrown popgun down if we're going to get me on my feet anytime soon. In fact, hand it over, I can use it as a crutch."

Reluctantly, Maudie handed her precious shotgun over. It had belonged to her grandmother. That, along with the old Franklin sewing machine, had been her sole inheritance from the woman who had helped raise her. "Don't stick the barrel down in the sand," she warned.

"Give me credit for half a brain, will you?" the man grumbled. Quickly, he broke the chamber. On finding it empty, he sent her a scathing look of disgust, braced the stock on the ground and held out his other hand.

Reluctantly, she took it.

Forty-five minutes later, Richmond Keegan was laid out like a planked mullet in a room beyond the room he had previously seen. He'd eyed an old kitchen table, but it had been too short. His reluctant hostess had solved the problem by laying a door on top of a daybed, and now he felt about as comfortable as it was possible for any man to feel when he was laid out with a broken back while a strange woman tiptoed around him sneaking suspicious looks at his body.

He muttered an introduction, but as it came out on the tail end of a groan, he wasn't sure she caught it. "What's your name, in case I have to ask you to notify my next of kin?"

"It's Maudie Winters. You can call me Ms. Winters, and you're not going to die here because that would be too complicated and I don't have time to mess with it."

Or him, Keegan interpreted. He would call her Mother Teresa if she could locate this damned muscle spasm and stomp on it with both feet, but for that he would have to turn over, and at the moment he'd rather eat raw possum than move a single muscle.

"I'd better go get your medicine. The sooner you're feeling better, the sooner you can go back."

Go back? Rich thought with bitter amusement. Inside the crumbling old ruin, where she'd obviously built herself a cozy little nest, he had been able to study her while she went about her business. It was either that or count the water stains on the ceiling. The irony of it was that she was the wrong type of woman to push all his buttons, yet she was doing it anyway. At least she would have been if she hadn't already incapacitated him.

"I'll need your keys. How do I locate your car?"

"Right-hand pocket. Marina parking lot. Connecticut plates. Other than one homemade rust bucket, it's the only thing on the lot."

She came closer, eyeing the bulge high on his right thigh. Seeing her hesitation, Keegan's lips curled in amusement.

"If you take something right away," she mumbled, "you'll probably be able to leave before dark. Um, could you—?"

"Sorry. Right now I can't even twitch an eyelid without agonizing pain." Which was something of an exaggeration. Pain, yeah. Agonizing, no—at least not after the first hour or so. "Miss Winters—"

Edging closer, she cautiously snaked her hand into his pants' pocket. The effect as her warm fingers burrowed down toward his groin was roughly equivalent to pulling about eight Gs.

She avoided his eyes, which told him that she hadn't been entirely unaffected by the intimate physical contact. "It's Mrs.," she mumbled.

Keegan was conscious of a flicker of disappointment. Just as well, though. He didn't need this kind of trouble, even if he'd been in any shape to enjoy it. "Mrs. Winters, it may come as unwelcome news, but I'm afraid you're going to be stuck with me for more than just a few hours. The last time this happened I was in bed for six days." Another exaggeration, but, hell—he might as well get whatever kicks he could out of the situation.

Maudie's jaw fell. "Six days! But you can't—that is, where will I—that is, I'd better go get your medicine!"

Keegan watched while she snatched a pair of sunglasses off the bronze bust of some dead composer and unhooked her coat from a funky-looking coatrack. "Bag's in the trunk," he said. "Look, I appreciate this, Mrs. Winters. Should I expect a—ah, Mr. Winters to show up while you're gone? This might be kind of hard to explain."

She looked startled. And then she shook her head and smiled, and damned if he didn't find himself smiling right back at her.

Remnants of the smile lingering after she'd left, Keegan began the mental exercise that had saved his sanity during the endless days and nights when he'd been held, severely injured, in a stinking hellhole with no company and not so much as a glimmer of light.

Essays. Tables. Anything and everything he had ever committed to memory.

One that had stuck by him since his school days, God knows why, had been something by Walter Scott. Under the circumstances, it seemed slightly more appropriate than Gaussian logarithms.

"'Soldier, rest! thy warfare o'er,'"

He grunted.

"'Sleep the sleep that knows not breaking:
Dream of... Dream of...' Oh, hell, dream of something! 'Days of danger, nights of...' Whatever.
'In our isle's enchanted hall...'"

He chuckled, and then winced at a fresh stab of pain. Hardly enchanted. At least, not this particular island's hall.

On the other hand, little Miss Frostbite was beginning to show definite signs of promise.

Two

Maudie took the twenty-five horsepower Evinrude rather than the little three-horse job she used when she was in no particular hurry. Today she was in a hurry. By the time she reached the marina and pulled into the small slip where she always tied up while she did her grocery shopping, collected her mail, checked with the real estate agent and visited her father, the sky had clouded up, making it seem later than it was.

"Visiting Medlin?" Jerry asked as he caught the bow-line, secured it and extended a hand.

"Not today." Not any day, if her father's new wife had anything to say about it, Maudie thought with only a remnant of regret. He was happy, though. That was all that mattered.

"Saw that fellow headed out your way this morning. Trouble?"

"Nothing I can't handle," she replied a bit grimly.

Maudie Winters was kin to half the people on the island, at least to the old original families. If Jerry had thought for a single moment that she needed help, he would have followed the stranger over. "I just need to get something out of his car, and then I'll be taking off again. Would you top off my can and put it on my tab?"

"Real gas guzzler you got there," said the cheerful youth as he reached down into the boat for her red gas can.

"It gets me around, don't knock it."

They both chuckled, and Maudie hurried around the building to the graveled parking lot, feeling better for the small exchange. She was not without friends. Quite the reverse. And while her father had taken himself a new wife, she still had her daughter. Ann Mary was away at school, but they were just as close as they'd always been, friends as well as mother and daughter.

Maudie valued her friends and family above all. She also valued her independence. For a woman who'd been a bride at eighteen and a divorced and penniless mother at twenty, she had managed to come about quite nicely. She had a more or less solid roof over her head, plenty of time for her painting and a year-round salaried position, something of a rarity in a place where most jobs were seasonal.

If she occasionally got hungry for the sound of another human voice in the winter months, all she had to do was come over to Hatteras. Or wait for the inevitable trespasser.

Quickly she hurried across the parking lot. In the past hour she had gone through feeling irritated, threatened and alarmed. A veritable emotional hurricane for a woman who prided herself on having an even disposition, but then Maudie had used up her lifetime allotment of anger twenty years ago, when Sanford Winters had told her he wasn't ready to start a family.

Neither had Maudie been ready, but they'd started one nonetheless, and Maudie wasn't a woman to quit a job half done. She had gone home to have her baby, while Sanford, using desertion as grounds, had started divorce proceedings. As he'd been a medical student living on a minuscule stipend and her clerk's pay at the time, he had agreed to establish a trust fund to be paid on their child's eighteenth birthday.

The same fund that was now paying Ann Mary's college expenses, Maudie thought with pride. Sanford had had his flaws—far more of them than she'd been aware of when she'd married him, a starry-eyed eighteen-year-old freshman, daughter of a commercial fisherman, working part-time in the college bookstore. But in the end, he had come through with the educational fund. It was all she'd ever asked of him, and all he'd ever offered.

As the pain in his back eased to a dull ache, Keegan began to take stock of his surroundings. When he'd entered the place before, he'd been far too conscious of the precarious state of the entire structure to do much exploring. The first door had led directly into a dark, cluttered room with half a dozen bowed two-by-fours supporting the sagging ceiling. With one eye to getting out before the entire works collapsed on his head, he had quickly raked a shelfful of books into several cartons, after emptying them of trash—mostly scraps of wood. There'd been two red glasses left incongruously on a battered old table. He had taken those and then gathered up the paintings that had been stacked near the door, as if left there to be collected at will by some leisurely thief.

He had tried the door at the back of the room and figured it was stuck. Otherwise he would have discovered her lair. In a former incarnation, the room had obviously been a kitchen. There was a porcelain sink on one wall, with no faucets and no drain. Its only function seemed to be as a repository of junk, which included an ugly life-size bust, several fishing reels in various states of disrepair, and a filthy—an *extremely* filthy—jelly jar. Nudged up alongside it was a galvanized sink with a pitcher pump and an odd arrangement of plumbing underneath that angled over beneath the porcelain job. Along the far wall between two disgracefully cloudy windows stood a rusty refrigerator, the kind with the compressor on top, and a two-eyed gas range, over which hung three blackened frying pans that looked as if they might have been a part of the original equipment.

There was a small, cast-iron stove with a few lengths of stovepipe venting out a covered window. It provided a touch of warmth, but Keegan didn't dare think about the safety factor.

Other than that, the dark paneled room was furnished with a few mismatched chairs, a wooden table, three stools and the daybed he was presently occupying. And while the walls and ceiling looked comparatively safe, the place was a dump. Hardly worth the trip south to investigate, and certainly not worth any more of his time.

As for the woman, he had the choice of running her out or—

Or what?

Richmond Keegan was an orderly man, both by nature and by training. Having grown up in a house with six younger siblings and an invalid mother, he had learned early that there was no middle ground between order and chaos.

This was a disorderly house. Which meant that Maudie Winters was—

Well, regardless of what she was, she was obviously just barely making it. God knows how she'd found the place, or how long she'd been squirreled up here. To protect his family from the very real possibility of a liability suit, he ought to turn her out.

On the other hand, she had to be in desperate need of a place to stay to have settled for a dump such as this. If he turned her out and she ended up completely homeless, he'd feel like a dog.

No, dammit! He wouldn't feel anything at all, because he wouldn't hang around long enough to see where she went from here.

Keegan reminded his conscience that he couldn't single-handedly save the world. The idealism that had driven him in his early years had been worn down to a weathered type of pragmatism that demanded a lot less emotional energy, which suited him just fine.

Men, he had come to realize, fought wars in which they wrought a path of destruction—killing, dying, taking prisoners and being taken prisoner. Occasionally good triumphed over evil. Temporarily, at least. But all too often, before the echo of the last cannon had even faded, viewpoints had shifted again and the world had moved on to the next great crisis.

Keegan had done his part, hoping, but never knowing, that he'd made a contribution to a better world. He'd done his share. He sure as hell wasn't obligated, even if he'd been in any position, to take on the care and feeding of a smart-mouthed female wielding a .410 that was theoretically loaded with double-ought buckshot.

A reluctant grin creased his leathery features. The feisty little baggage hadn't once raised her voice. No more than five feet two at the most, probably about a hundred pounds soaking wet, armed only with an empty popgun and a cool-as-green-ice look on her face, and she hadn't thought twice about tackling a hundred ninety-nine pounds of trained fighting machine.

Keegan admired guts. The little lady had 'em, in spades. So maybe he would let her stay. He could afford to be generous, it was no skin off his nose. In a few months this wouldn't even be Keegan property any longer, although liability-wise, he wasn't quite sure of the status of this crumbling old ruin once the property it was built on reverted to its original owner.

With the situation awareness that had made him not only a top pilot but an outstanding officer, Keegan examined and evaluated the evidence. She was not a Keegan; therefore she was trespassing, because this was definitely his grandfather's old place. The weathered name plate in which the carved letters spelling out Keegan's Hunt were still legible was mounted on one of the leaning walls on the other side.

If he ran her out, she could be homeless. On the other hand, she could be killed if he let her stay. Or she could be injured and then bankrupt every Keegan heir for the next three generations with a whopping liability suit. Which she would probably win, being a woman.

Being a small, shapely, helpless, appealing woman who smelled of soap and sunshine and clover—a woman with a dimple in her rounded little chin and wispy silken eyebrows winging over a pair of sea-green eyes, with a soft, husky voice and—

Oh, hell.

All right, so it might be a good idea if he hung around a few days and sort of policed up the place for her. He could shore up a few walls—maybe replace those flimsy two-bys with four-by-fours and check to be sure the roof wasn't about to collapse. Nothing major, Keegan told himself, just enough to see her through until she could get on her feet and find herself a better place to stay.

He might even find a tactful way to leave her a little grocery money, something for emergencies. A woman obviously down on her luck could always use a helping hand, and it wasn't as if he had anything better to do with his time. It had been pretty obvious that his family had wanted him to shove off for a while.

The trouble was, he kept forgetting that while he'd been away in the service, they'd been growing up and establishing families of their own.

Which was the way it should be, Keegan told himself. Only it took a little time to adjust to all the changes. He hadn't even got the hang of being a civilian again after half a lifetime in uniform.

Having dozed briefly on the door-daybed contraption, Keegan was well into plans for making Maudie's life easier when he heard the muted putt-putt of a small outboard. He should have insisted she use his rental instead of that heavy old clunker tied up at the pier. At least then she wouldn't be out gas money on his behalf.

He glanced at his chronometer. She'd been gone less than an hour. Funny—it had seemed longer. A lot longer.

"Got it," she said a few minutes later, bringing in a burst of cold, salt-marsh-smelling air with faint overtones of rain and outboard fuel.

"I'll reimburse you."

She looked puzzled. "For the bag? Don't be silly."

"For the gas. And the time, of course."

Her face settled into an expression he was fast coming to recognize. She peeled off her thick parka and hung it on the tripod arrangement of galvanized pipes. "That's not necessary," she said with a calmness he was also coming to recognize.

He knew the type, having run across it more than once in Third World countries. Neediness and vulnerability wrapped up in enough pride to choke a camel.

Or break a man's heart.

She placed the battered leather flight bag beside him and turned to the refrigerator. "Do you need something to take it with?"

"First I'll need a hand digging it out. That is, unless you enjoy watching a grown man cry."

She narrowed her eyes at him, and Keegan wondered if he was laying it on too thick. His muscle spasms, when they hit, hurt like hell, but before he'd left the hospital the therapist had showed him how to roll a tennis ball under his back and use his own weight to knead the area until the spasm released. Lacking the ball, he had used his fist, which had worked pretty well, although the strain of getting it under there had brought a chilling sweat to his entire body.

Watching him from the corner of her eye, Maudie unzipped the bag, hoping the medicine would be right on top. She didn't relish pawing through a stranger's personal belongings. She liked it even less once she saw the way he packed. Her ex-husband had been a neatness freak, too.

"Can't find it? Should be right on top."

How on earth had his socks survived being tossed in and out of her boat without breaking formation? They were lined up in five neat rolls, with a stack of handkerchiefs and a tennis ball—a *tennis ball?*—at one end and a shaving kit at the other. "A place for everything and everything in its place," she muttered.

"You got a problem with that?"

"With what?"

"Everything in its place."

"It's not my problem," she replied, implying that it was his.

Irritated, he said, "The pills are in my shaving kit."

Naturally, it was a fitted one. She refrained from comment. Maudie appreciated neatness and organization as much as the next person, but she had her own system. It had to do with making the most of what she had, keeping her priorities straight, and never mind appearances.

She found the pill bottle, glanced at the label, and read off, "'Richmond Keegan, Col., USAF.' That's you?"

"My apologies for not rising. I'll curtsy twice tomorrow."

Lips twitching against a smile, she handed him the pill bottle, poured him a glass of water, and when he looked as if he might break his neck trying to take it without drowning, she slid a supporting arm under his shoulders.

"Easy," he said, wincing, and she bit her lip. Intruder or not, she could never deliberately inflict pain on anyone.

His head was heavy. It was warm, and she told herself that it was also exceedingly hard. His military cut, dark blond and salted with gray, had grown out enough to reveal several cowlicks, and she'd be willing to bet that his hairline was higher than it had been a few years ago.

She tried her best not to watch while he swallowed the dose, but it was impossible not to notice certain things. Such as the jarring masculinity of him. Such as the startling blue of his eyes and the lines that did nothing to diminish the attractiveness of his weathered features.

He was hurting, but he covered it well. Without knowing a thing about the man, she was certain that he had more control than was good for him. Probably had ulcers, too. His kind usually did.

"How long do you think it will be before you can leave?" she asked.

"Hospitable little thing, aren't you?" He wiped off the moisture from his mouth, and Maudie found herself unable to look away. He had slipped off his leather jacket just before she had laid him out on the door, and with his broad shoulders flattened against the hard surface, his chest looked positively massive in the crisp blue shirt. Nor did the fact that he was lying down instead of towering over her do much to minimize the fact that he was too entirely big, entirely too masculine, entirely too—

Too everything Maudie didn't need in her carefully ordered life.

"I'm sorry, Colonel Keegan, but—"

"Richmond," he corrected. "Or Rich, if you prefer."

Her lips tightened, irritation flashing in her eyes. "In case it escaped your notice, Colonel Keegan, my guest facilities are rather limited. If you'd like, I can take you back across in your rental, and Jerry can bring me home."

"Home?"

"Back here. Do you have a problem with that?" She turned his phrase against him, and Keegan had to grin.

Maudie looked away. It *wasn't* an attractive grin, and he *wasn't* an attractive man, and she wasn't the *least bit* curious about what a colonel in the air force was doing lying on a door across her daybed smack-dab in the middle of January.

"Mrs. Winters, we need to have a little talk about who belongs here and who doesn't, but if it's all the same to you, I'd as soon leave it for another day."

Maudie's eyes widened. "I just told you—"

"And I told *you* that I'm not going anywhere any time soon. That I can guarantee, lady, so if you don't care to share space, then you'd better start making other arrangements. I understand there are several more houses on this island. Maybe if you got started picking locks while there's still enough daylight left to see by, you could be all moved in by dark.''

Maudie's jaw fell, revealing a row of even white teeth that showed to advantage against her olive complexion. "I'm sure you could tell me exactly how to go about it. Housebreaking seems to be a specialty of yours. But you see, Colonel, I happen to have a perfectly good bed all made up with clean sheets and three warm quilts. Why should I want to break into a cold, damp house where the rooms haven't even been aired in months?''

Without moving a muscle, he gave the appearance of shrugging. "Suit yourself. If you don't mind sharing, I'm sure I can handle it.'' His gaze dropped appraisingly down her voluptuous little body, lingering on the feminine swell of her breasts under two visible layers of shirt before moving on to survey the ripe flare of her hips in the faded blue jeans. Something glinted in his eyes, like sunlight catching a shifting shoal of finger mullet. "I can pretty well guarantee I won't be much of a threat to you. At least, not tonight.''

Maudie couldn't remember the last time she'd lost her temper. She was determined not to let him get under her skin, because she had a pretty good idea he was deliberately trying to do just that.

Her ex-husband had been a master at manipulation. Being able to make her lose control had done a lot for Sanford's twisted ego. It had taken her twenty-six months of marriage and a lot of pain before she had figured that out. "Would you care for a cup of coffee?'' she asked, determined to swallow her irritation if it poisoned her.

"I'd care for a lot more than that, but I'll settle for coffee.''

And when she spun around to glare at him, he said mildly, "I skipped breakfast this morning, and—"

"That's hardly my fault."

"—by now, it must be nearly dinnertime."

"I'll make you a sandwich and open a can of soup. Can you eat it lying down without choking?"

"I'll try. You can always roll me over and beat me on the shoulders."

This time she was certain of it. That grin of his was lethal!

Over canned soup and grilled-cheese sandwiches, made in one of those godawful frying pans of hers that had at least an inch of black crust burned onto the outside, Keegan explained his mission.

"So you see, the lease runs out in a couple of months, anyway. I just drove down to see if there was anything worth salvaging. I've got a lot of family. One of these days, the kids might appreciate something that once belonged to a great or a great-great ancestor."

He had family, Maudie thought with a pang of regret all out of proportion to the event. What did she care? He was only a stranger. A man who looked as if he'd been hacked out of teakwood with a chain saw. A man who didn't know the difference between a contemporary acrylic painting and something his grandfather might have collected. Who needed him?

"You can have the bust and whatever furniture you can drag out that was here originally, although I warn you, most of it's been wet so many times it's not worth the effort. The older parts of the house suffered a lot of damage back in the forties and fifties. We had some bad storms then."

"You can hardly be speaking from personal experience," Keegan said in a blatant ploy to discover her age. She could be anywhere between mid-twenties and mid-thirties. She had the kind of beauty—light brown hair, olive skin, great bone structure despite her diminutive size—that defied aging.

Maudie made another pot of coffee. While they'd been talking, it had grown completely dark outside. Wind howled around the old house, making it seem snug by contrast, although there were drafts that made the layering of clothes imperative. "There haven't been near as many storms in recent years. Something to do with cycles, I think. Or rainfall on some desert or other."

Rich let his imagination off the leash. Something about the woman got to him, although he'd be hard put to say just why. "Your grandfather owned land on Coronoke, right?"

"My great-grandfather."

"Right. And your parents still live over on Hatteras?"

"My father and his new wife."

The stepmother. That might explain a few things. "Your folks own the other cottages?"

"Don't I wish. My family once owned the whole island, but gradually they sold off pieces. Some just washed away. It was my great-grandfather who leased the club site to yours, I suppose, but I know my grandfather hunted over here. And Daddy worked over here as a hunting guide when he was about thirteen or so."

"That young?"

"It was probably illegal, but nobody reported him. He was too good at it. He stayed on as a sort of caretaker long after the hunters stopped coming down. I don't think he was paid for it, but he had a vested interest, you might say."

"I guess we both have an interest," Keegan said after the silence had stretched out for several minutes. He still didn't feel comfortable about leaving her there unprotected. What if he'd been some kind of a creep? What if there was another bad storm? What if she got sick?

"You're not, uh, here on vacation?" he asked, knowing she wasn't. If her father lived over on Hatteras, why would she spend her vacation in a dump such as this practically within sight of her home?

The stepmother? Somehow, he couldn't see Ms. Winters allowing herself to be chased out of her home by another woman. She had taken him on, hadn't she? A combat-hardened, hot-tempered stranger, and she'd challenged him without even batting an eyelash. If he'd been anyone else, she could have been in a lot of trouble.

His gaze followed her calm, graceful movements as she rose and crossed to the stove. After adjusting the damper, she shut the bottom door and spread her hands over the top.

The temperature outside had been in the low fifties earlier—warm for January. Inside, it must be all of sixty. And falling.

A brief memory of what a hacking cough had done to him when his back was at its worst, while he'd been held prisoner with no access to medical treatment, nearly made him reconsider his decision to stay.

"All right, then," she said, sounding resigned. "I suppose you can either sleep here or take the bed in the guest room. My daughter sleeps there when she visits."

Guest room? She entertained *guests* in this dump?

Her *daughter!* "As long as it's bigger than a crib, I'll take it."

She sent him a skeptical look. "Do you think you can manage to move?"

"If you can help me sit up, I can make it the rest of the way under my own steam."

Steam, as it turned out, was not far off the mark. By the time she had ducked her head under his arm, brushing his face with a mop of windblown hair that looked like silk and smelled like clover—by the time her surprisingly voluptuous breasts were pressed against his side so that she could lever him into a sitting position, Keegan was about ready to surrender.

Jeez! He'd known he was deficient in vitamin S, but he hadn't known he was this bad off! Given the fact that he'd been at war—on standby a lot longer than that—and either in captivity or hospitalized for a hell of a lot longer than even that, he hadn't had much time to remedy the deficiency.

Not that he had ever been promiscuous, either before or after his brief marriage, but he was a pilot, after all. Pilots were known for their alpha libidos. And little Mrs. Winters was a small, explosive bundle of high-powered temptation.

Unfortunately, he was in no condition at the moment to light her fuse. Much less enjoy the explosion.

The room he was shown was about six feet wide and twenty-four feet long. God knows what it had been originally. All he was concerned about at the moment was that the walls were more or less vertical, the ceiling and floor more or less horizontal, and there was a bed in one corner that looked about as soft as a marble tomb, if considerably warmer. And that there was a hurricane candle on the wall shelf.

There was a bathroom, too, some parts of which were actually operational. Damned good thing! He was in no shape to go stumbling around in search of a privy.

He leaned stiffly against the door frame until his reluctant hostess provided him with a towel and washcloth. "I'm afraid the bathtub doesn't work," she said. As it was currently the repository of several miles of monofilament net, he wasn't particularly surprised. "We heat water on the stove and use the lavatory or a washtub."

Great. He would have given half his retirement pay for thirty minutes in a Jacuzzi right now, jets going full blast.

"No problem."

Big problem, but what the hell—he hadn't come here to wallow in the lap of luxury.

"Then if that's all you need—?"

It wasn't, but he didn't figure she was interested in supplying what it was he did need. Nor had he known he needed it until a short while ago. Keegan figured it was going to be a long night, and the sooner he got started on it, the sooner it would be over.

The bed felt damp and cold, and unfortunately, he wasn't sleepy. Too much coffee. Too much to think about. Besides, it was barely 2100 hours, and he never went to bed before the late news. From what he could see, there wasn't a newsstand on the island, much less a TV. How did anyone around here keep up with what was going on in the world? Did they even care?

It had been a rotten idea, coming down to look over a property that was going to pass out of his family's hands in a matter of weeks. Dismissing the real reasons for the trip south, Keegan figured he would give it another day, inspect the place for the most obvious dangers, and then head north again.

Okay, maybe a couple of days, but that was all. He had a life to get on with. He had a future to plan. It was time he started exploring the career possibilities open to a broken-down ex-fighter pilot with no job experience outside the military. Not that he needed the money. He had invested carefully over the years, and outside of a few personal extravagances—he appreciated precision engineering, whether it was wings, wheels, or a chronometer—his life-style was simple to the extreme. At least it was now that an extravagant wife was no longer a part of it.

The problem, Keegan decided, was that he was constitutionally incapable of being idle for more than a short period of time. His family had sent him on this wild-goose chase in the first place because as much as they cared for him—and he didn't doubt that they did—they didn't particularly want him running their lives any longer. Which left him with—

While Keegan pondered the options open to a forty-two-year-old man who was no longer in peak physical condition, and who had no job experience in the civilian world, a gust of wind struck the side of the rambling old ruin, causing timbers to groan and creak. Rain slashed against weathered old walls, sending drafts fingering through the single boarded-up window. He pulled the stack of heavy quilts up closer under his chin.

Which left him with—

"Ah, jeez," he muttered, wiping away the drop of water that struck his left cheek and dribbled down into his ear. "A leaky roof."

Three

By the time Maudie rapped on the door and entered, Keegan had dodged leaks until he'd given up. Huddling on a stool in the corner of the room, under the dryest of the three lumpy quilts, he scowled at the flashlight. "You brought the lifeboat, I presume?"

"Sorry about this. Ann Mary usually bunks in with me when it rains."

"If that's an invitation—"

"It's not. I forgot I'd moved her bed over to repair the floor underneath. You want the daybed again?"

"With or without the door?"

"Your choice." Other than a tendency to shiver, she seemed perfectly composed, and her very calmness struck him on the raw.

Dim light from the room beyond—about a twenty-five-watt job, he estimated—was just enough to halo her hair around her head, not enough to put a strain on the generator that supplied power to the Hunt. "A door on a daybed. Is that the best you can do?" he grumbled.

"I'm offering you a dry place to sleep, Colonel Keegan. You're free to take it or leave."

Thus spake the Grand Duchess of Coronoke, he thought with grudging admiration. Aloud he said, "I'm much obliged to you, ma'am."

"You needn't be. According to you, it's your roof."

"According to me? I thought we'd hashed all that out. Are you saying now you doubt my word?"

"I don't doubt that you're a Keegan. That doesn't necessarily mean you're descended from the same bunch of Keegans that built the Hunt."

The planes of his face seemed to flatten out, giving him the look of a big predatory cat. "What happened in the last hour or so to make you change your mind?" he purred.

"I haven't changed it. I simply hadn't finished making it up."

"You took me in."

"I could hardly leave you lying on the beach, bleeding all over my island." She had a way of smiling that made the Mona Lisa look like a circus clown.

"Dammit, I wasn't bleeding!" he exploded.

Maudie lifted a cool eyebrow, her very calmness giving her an advantage. "No?"

Swearing, Keegan socked a fist in his palm, causing his quilts to slip, causing him to have to grab them. Causing him to swear even harder.

"You're repeating yourself, Colonel. I'd have thought you'd been in the service long enough to have developed a more extensive vocabulary. Do you want the daybed, or don't you?"

When he didn't reply immediately, Maudie returned to the living room, which also happened to be her kitchen, dining room, tackle repair shop and studio. Uncomfortably aware of her thirteen-year-old bathrobe and the draggle of flowered flannel drooping beneath the hem, she made a deliberate effort to elongate her body. Dignity, her father always used to say, was in the bearing, not in the height.

The colonel blew out his candle and followed her. Maudie told herself that a man his size and temperament should have looked ludicrous draped in a church bazaar quilt. Oddly enough, he didn't. Richmond Keegan had a certain dignity about him—a certain air of authority that came through in the way he carried himself. Her father had been right.

Of course, part of it might be due to the fact that he was about a foot taller than she was, with the kind of build most men only dreamed of. With or without his clothes, it occurred to her that Colonel Keegan just might be a bit more dangerous than she'd first thought.

"If you need another pillow, you may have one of mine." She deliberately made her tone impersonal in case he got the idea that she was offering to share more than her personal bedding with him.

"Thanks. I'll do without."

She shrugged. "Suit yourself," she murmured, and was halfway to the door of her own room when he spoke again.

"You saving the rest of that coffee for morning?"

The pot was about a third full. "No," she said, although if he hadn't asked, she would have reheated it for breakfast.

"Mind if I have some?"

"Be my guest." A gust of rain slashed the windows just as a shutter slammed loudly against the wall. Maudie ignored it. Keegan reacted as if he'd been shot.

"Don't worry, it's only the shutter," she reassured him. "I keep them fastened back, but sometimes the hooks pull out of the wood."

It banged again. A branch rubbed a corner of the roof. Maudie was used to the sounds of the old house, but evidently the colonel had a problem with nerves. In which case, the last thing he needed was another jolt of her high-test coffee.

But that was his problem, not hers. "Good night, then, Colonel," she said calmly, and turned once more to her own cozy bedroom.

"I may as well go ahead and fix the damned thing, or else neither one of us'll get any sleep tonight," he grumbled.

"Right now? But it's raining."

"Where do you keep your tools?"

Oh, great. Colonel Macho to the rescue, just what she needed. Maudie had been up since before daybreak. She was tired. People days—days when she either went to Hatteras or had to deal with visitors on Coronoke, legitimate or otherwise—wore her out. Today she had had to deal with both. Was still dealing.

"All right, all right, then move aside. I'll just close it from inside until morning." She tried to reach around him. Like a light-blinded stag, he just stood there. "Excuse me?"

"If you open it now, you'll flood the place! The rain's coming from this side, in case you hadn't noticed!"

"I noticed. You're the one who can't take a little banging shutter."

"And I'm the one who offered to fix it!"

"Oh, sure—waltz out there in the middle of the night with your broken back and—"

"It's not broken!" he shouted.

"No? That wasn't why you were practically crawling on your hands and knees this afternoon?"

The look he sent her could have sliced through concrete. "I had a muscle spasm, all right? There's nothing wrong with me!"

"Other than your disposition, you mean?"

"Dammit all to hell, lady, there's not a damned thing wrong with my disposition! Now, are you going to tell me where the hell you keep your tools, or am I going to have to go out there and wrench the damned thing off the side of the house with my bare hands?"

"Why don't you just . . . breathe on it?" Maudie smiled sweetly. Taking a plastic tarp off a shelf, she unrolled it, spread it on the floor in front of the window and raised the lower sash. Wind howled into the room like a herd of dragons. A stack of papers scattered across the floor. One of the canvases that she had retrieved from the boat house just before dark toppled over, and Keegan, clutching his flapping quilt more tightly around him, began to swear again.

In less than a minute, she had caught the banging shutter, pulled it shut and hooked it on the inside. "There— that'll hold it until morning, unless this hook pulls out, too. Old wood doesn't have much gripping power." Deftly, she rolled up the rain-spattered tarp and shoved it behind the bust on the porcelain drainboard.

His look said he'd like to grip her, right around her skinny little neck. Maudie ignored the skitter of nerves that raced down her spine. "Help yourself to the coffee, Colonel Keegan." Smiling, she turned toward her bedroom. Again.

"Mrs. Winters!"

Maudie halted. She didn't turn around. He might be a colonel, but he had the bark of a drill sergeant. "Yes—sir?"

"Would you mind telling me something?"

"If I can. Sir."

"Lady, I can take all the insolence you can dish out, if it makes you feel one damned bit better."

"I'm glad to hear it." Her fingernails would have been digging into her palms if she didn't keep them trimmed short. The man irritated the blue blazes out of her, and Maudie Winters didn't have an irritable bone in her body!

"Why didn't you just ask me to fix the shutter? Is that such a big deal? You have to show off your independence, is that it? You're one of these women who has to prove she's as good as any man?"

Slowly she turned and looked him directly in the eye—and then wished she hadn't. His eyes were distractingly beautiful. The last thing she needed now was distraction. "I don't have to prove it. In the first place, Colonel, I—"

"The name is Rich."

"As I was saying, in the first place, I—"

"Say it."

"Say what?"

"Say my name, dammit!"

Maudie's slippered left foot began to tap. "In the first place, Colonel Keegan, I am both accustomed to and capable of looking after myself and my home." She waited to see if he intended to challenge her on that home business. When he didn't, she went on. "As for being independent, anyone with half a brain would know better than to go messing around outside an old house with the wind blowing a gale. Shingles come sailing off the roof with a velocity you wouldn't believe. Besides which, even if you'd nailed the shutter to the wall, I'd just have to pry it loose again when I needed to close it against a real storm. The wood's in bad enough shape without my having to use a pry bar on it."

He started to speak, but she overrode him. Maudie was calm by nature. A doormat, she was not. "Furthermore, those old sashes are heavy. If you'd tried to lift it, you'd probably have set your back off again, and then I'd have been forced to stay up the rest of the night nursing you, and—"

"That'll be the day," he jeered.

"And I have better things to do with my time. As to how you spend yours, that's your business. Good night, Colonel Keegan."

Rich watched her disappear behind the watermarked walnut door. He counted down from fifty and found it inadequate. He was still steamed. What *was* it with women these days? Even his own sisters were suddenly too proud to admit they needed his help!

The Winters woman needed help, all right, but first he was going to have to figure out some way to get past that hedgehog pride of hers. Because that's all it was, pride. There was no other reason possible for any thinking person to refuse help when help was so obviously needed.

Dammit, he wasn't trying to put her down. He *liked* women! He even admired their independence—up to a point. But any fool knew that men were physically stronger than women. God had designed them that way for a purpose! Women were supposed to be the nurturers, men the protectors and providers.

Only now, all of a sudden, the whole damned female half of the species seemed determined to deny the natural order of things!

"Well, not on *my* watch," he muttered. Reaching into his bag, he removed a stiffly starched uniform shirt, rolled it up and placed it exactly eighteen inches from the top of the door, which was still resting on top of the daybed. Then he marched back into his leaking bedroom and snatched up the pillow. Turning it dry side up, he placed it precisely where the bend of his knees would come on the door. Then carefully he lowered himself onto the flat surface, neck on the rolled shirt, the bend of his knees on the pillow. He pressed the small of his back against the rigid oak and drew the quilt up under his chin.

Ten minutes later he was still staring up at the ceiling, wondering what made women so devilishly determined to prove they could do without a man. A man, hell! Without *him!* First it had been Alice. Then his sisters and sisters-in-law. Now this little snip of a thing, with her great green eyes and her antique firearm—!

Eventually he must have slept, because later he remembered waking sometime in the night to discover that the rain had stopped beating against the house. The wind was no more than a plaintive sigh.

Another day. He'd give her one more day.

"You'll be wanting to get on back," Maudie said over fresh coffee, bacon and French toast the next morning. She was wearing jeans again, with layers on the top. He counted three of them, including a pink turtleneck, a black wool pullover and a paint-stained flannel shirt.

None of which obscured her voluptuous little body, to Keegan's regret.

"I'm in no hurry." Flexing his shoulders, he ignored the dull ache in the small of his back, which was all that was left of yesterday's muscle spasm.

"Yes, well . . . I suppose that's up to you, but don't expect me to play hostess. I have too much to do to wait around while you make up your mind."

"Make up my mind about what?"

Which was she, Keegan wondered, the dewy-faced schoolgirl she resembled, or the mature, sensual woman he knew her to be? There was a guardedness about her that told him she wasn't as young as he'd first thought. She was probably closer to thirty-five, give or take a few years. Interesting age. Young enough to appreciate her own maturity.

And his?

His eyes strayed to her lips, glistening just now with butter and syrup, and his entire train of thought was abruptly derailed. She licked the butter off her lips, and he felt a film of sweat bead his brow. "You, uh, you wanted me to make up my mind about something?"

"About what you want to take back to your family?"

"My family. Right. So we're finally agreed that the house is mine?"

"I never said it wasn't."

"You gave a pretty good try at booting me off the island. And then, last night—"

"Ah, but the island isn't yours." Maudie sipped her coffee and did her best to ignore the presence of the large, ruggedly attractive man at her table. He made waves. By simply existing, he made waves. "I've decided to grant you the house. Even if you're not the right branch of Keegans, you've probably got more of a claim than I have."

"Magnanimous concession," he murmured, eyes glinting with restored good humor.

"Understand, I'm not offering to move out, I'm only conceding that you might be related to the people who built the place a hundred years ago."

"Ninety-nine."

"Whatever. So... now that you've come, you've seen and you've conquered, I expect you'll be anxious to get back to wherever it is you live?"

"Connecticut. North of Hartford. And I'm in no hurry."

"Yes, well... take your time. I'll be leaving in a few minutes. I have things to do on the other end of the island, but if I can help you with anything before I go—like carrying stuff down to your boat—just ask. The old things are yours, the new ones are mine. I'll just have to trust you to know the difference, because I have work to do."

"You mentioned the bust. Was it here when you moved in?"

Maudie glanced at the battered fake bronze wearing her sunglasses. "You mean Joe? You don't think I'd go out and buy something that ugly, do you?" She sipped her coffee, took another bite of toast and grinned, and Keegan was struck again by her unusual appeal. He'd finally figured it out. There was nothing fake about her. She simply was what she was.

And he was rapidly coming to appreciate what she was.

"Joe, huh?" He examined the thing again. One ear was missing. The nose and one eyebrow had been severly damaged. Judging from the looks, it had fallen on its face more than a few times.

"Joe Bach. I thought at first Beethoven, but the hairline's all wrong. Of course, with the missing ear, it might even be van Gogh, but he looks more musical than arty, don't you think?"

Keegan's knowledge of classical music was on a par with his knowledge of art. "Joe it is, then. Since you two are on a first-name basis, I guess you'd better keep him."

"You don't think your children will mind?"

"My children, if I had any, wouldn't know, so how could they mind?"

"I thought you said you had children."

"Not me. If I mentioned children, I was probably referring to my nieces and nephews. About a dozen of 'em, all living within twenty-five miles of each other."

"You must be a close family," she observed, and Keegan shot her a searching look. Was that a wistful note he'd detected? Ms. Independence had a flaw in her case-hardened armor?

"Yeah, I guess. Look, how about I spend the morning inspecting this place, and then maybe I'll run over and stock up on whatever we need for the next few days?"

Maudie's jaw dropped in a delicate expression of disbelief. "Whatever we need for *what?*"

"Food, for starters. Tools, repair materials. Is there a lumber supply place on the island? How about a hardware store?"

"Whoa. Just back up a minute there, Colonel." She stood up, raking her stool back, and held up one small, shapely hand, palm outward. Keegan could see the row of calluses at the base of each finger. There was a cut on her little finger, a smear of green paint ingrained in the skin of her thumb. "If you're worried about that shutter, then don't. I have my own system. You may rest assured I'll take care of it before the next wind, and if you're worried about—"

"I'm not worried, as you put it, about anything, Maudie. While I'm here, I mean to do my level best to see that this place doesn't cave in on top of you while you're living here. My family can do without a lawsuit, and these days, No Trespassing signs are no defence."

"Tell me about it."

"So, as I said, I'm going to look the place over first, make out a requisition—that is, a shopping list of what's needed for immediate repairs. While I'm at it, I'll see about reprovisioning."

"Oh, no. No meddling with my house, and—"

"Whose house?"

"And no reprovisioning, if you mean what I think you mean. There's nothing I need from you, Colonel Ke—"

"Dammit, the name is Rich! Say it! It won't kill you to unbend that much, will it?"

He was ranting again, and Maudie shrugged. She had never seen such a short fuse on any man. "Whatever. But I don't want you crawling all over my house—"

"*My* house!"

"*Our* house, then. It's safe enough, or else I'd never allow my daughter to set foot in it, and besides—"

"If you really have a daughter and this place is so safe, why isn't she living here with you, answer me that if you can?"

He had a jaw like the cowcatcher on an old steam locomotive. "For the very good reason that she's away at school."

"On Hatteras?"

"No, at college."

"Your daughter's in *college?*"

"Yes, Colonel Keegan, my daughter is in college. Believe it or not, we Outer Bankers are a fairly literate people." Maudie was having a bit of trouble hanging on to her own temper, and that wasn't like her. Normally she was the most tolerant of women, but this overgrown, overweening, overbearing tin soldier needed taking down a few pegs, and she was sorely tempted to tackle the job! "The reason I don't want you climbing all over my house, Colonel, is that I don't want to see you get hurt again. Not on my island. I don't have time to waste looking after you, and while I'm just as sorry as I can be about what happened yesterday, it was your own fault for barging in without even notifying me first."

She could have sworn that his cheekbones flattened out again. His eyes had a decidedly feral glint to them, but when he didn't argue, she nodded her head in acceptance of *his* acceptance of guilt and went on with her statement. "The thing is, Colonel Keegan, a man with your lack of coordination has no business messing around a place like this. It can be dangerous if you don't know what you're doing, and you obviously don't. If you're not familiar with which parts of the house are sound and which aren't, you'll wind up falling through the floor, I'll have to pull you out, and quite frankly, I have better things to do with my time than to keep hauling you out of trouble. And furthermore—" But she couldn't think of a single furthermore. "And—well, that's all I have to say."

Oh, yes, he definitely had the flat-faced look again, all sharp-edged planes and half-closed eyes. She'd seen the very same look once on a big, tawny cat at the Ashboro Zoo. "So now, if you don't mind, Colonel, I'll say good-bye."

He was around the table before she could take a second step. Towering over her, he was so close she could see the edge of a very crisply ironed shirt. Suddenly he was all around her, surrounding her, as if he were the very air she breathed. She took a step back, and he stepped right with her. Her right leg, his left one.

"The name is Rich," he said so softly it was little more than a rumbling purr. "Say it."

Her eyes slid away. She was suddenly nervous. Maudie was *never* nervous! "Please—" she whispered.

"Say my name."

"What difference can it possibly make whether or not I—"

The air between them held enough electricity to jump-start a B-12 bomber. The instant before his arms came around her, Maudie could have sworn every hair on her body stood up. He lifted her off her feet and his mouth absorbed whatever protest she might have made.

She forgot to breathe. There wasn't enough air in the room, even if she'd remembered. Her last fleeting thought was that it was only flesh on flesh. Two sets of lips. No big deal. But she knew better than that, even before the thought slipped her mind.

It was a big deal. Whatever it had begun as, the kiss swiftly accelerated into a hunger that fed on itself as fiercely as any forest fire.

Maudie's small fists beat a few impotent tattoos on his chest and then slid like melted candle wax down his washboard stomach to catch on his belt. She was swamped by sensations of heat, of hardness, of strength. He tasted of coffee and some exotic masculine essence she couldn't begin to define—something far more intoxicating than her uncle Buster's homemade scuppernong wine.

At the first electrifying touch of his tongue, she dug her fingers under his belt and hung on while the earth shifted like quicksand under her feet. Maudie couldn't remember the last time she had been kissed. Really kissed. How could she have forgotten this power, this wild, sweet compulsion that could spring up out of nowhere to drown out every vestige of common sense?

Because it never happened to you before, that's why!

Never. Not like this.

Oh, Lord, why hadn't she simply picked up her tools and walked out? Why hadn't she quit while she was ahead?

Four

Incredible, Maudie thought distractedly, that a mouth that looked so hard could feel so soft. Soft, firm, warm—tasting of coffee and some mysterious essence that could quickly become addictive....

"Why'd you do that?" she gasped when she could speak again.

"Why?" His voice sounded as if it had been strained through burlap. "Because I wanted to and couldn't think of a single reason why not." Not a single reason but a thousand reasons, Keegan added silently, already regretting the impulse. He was not an impulsive man. Quick tempered, quick acting, quick thinking, but never impulsive.

Oh, no? Then why the hell did you do it?

Just showing her who's in charge around here.

Yeah. Right.

Go to hell, Keegan.

Maudie was aware of several things at once. A certain look in Keegan's flame-blue eyes that was blanked out almost instantly. The sudden weakness of her own knees. An obscure sense of disappointment that it was over so soon—which, of course, she immediately rejected.

Struggling to regain her composure, she said, "Well—at least you've got it out of your system."

He growled something unintelligible in response.

It was just a kiss. A simple kiss! It was hardly the first time a man had kissed her. The trouble was, when the man doing the kissing was Rich Keegan, there was nothing simple about it.

"So... I guess I'll say goodbye," Maudie said finally, with every appearance of composure. "I have at least half a day's work waiting on the other side of the island, and after that—" After that... what?

Only the rest of her life. Only more years of checking for mice and leaky plumbing, repairing broken shutters, mending torn screens and replacing missing shingles. Of talking to racoons, watching the seasons pass, the weather change. Haunting the post office waiting for Ann Mary's infrequent letters and watching her own hair turn gray.

She drew in a deep, shuddering breath and gave him her Sunday best smile with no way of knowing that it had the power to rock him back on his heels. "I reckon I'd better get on with it, then."

Bracing himself against the combined force of a pair of cool green eyes and a blinding white smile, Keegan swore silently. He told himself no woman was all that unflappable. He told himself she irritated the hell out of him. He told himself that for two bits, he would grab her and—!

Dammit, didn't *anything* get a rise out of her? He could have sworn she'd been just as shaken as he was by that kiss they'd shared. Every system in his body had pegged well into the red.

He stepped back, and so did she. Under that cool facade, she looked wary. He hadn't meant to frighten her—he would never deliberately frighten any woman. But, dammit, what did it take to make an impression on her?

He watched her duck into her bedroom and shut the door, and he stood there staring at the stains and scars on what had once been an elegant piece of millwork in an elegant hunting lodge.

The place was a ruin now, and God help him, he wasn't in much better shape. He was still standing there when she emerged again, wearing the down jacket that should have have made her look dumpy but somehow didn't.

"When you're through with breakfast, if there's anything left over, how about putting it into the refrigerator? I save scraps."

"Sure, no problem."

I save scraps? As in leftovers, sure—but plate scraps? If she had a pet, he'd missed it. She didn't have one. Probably couldn't afford one. So maybe, he thought as the door closed quietly behind her, he could get her one. A dog, maybe. A big one. With a year's supply of chow.

Oh, hell. He had probably devoured a week's worth of her groceries in one sitting! Half a dozen slices of bacon, half a dozen more slices of her rich, eggy French toast swimming in butter and syrup. Coffee wasn't cheap, either, and he'd been hitting her supply pretty heavily. As with most of the fighter pilots he knew, caffeine was the fuel of choice.

Keegan spared himself a moment for guilt, but guilt wasn't a feeling he wore comfortably. Or for long. When something was wrong, he fixed it. It was that simple.

Order of the day: complete safety inspection of premises, followed by the requisition of materials necessary to bring premises up to grade. She had taken a small toolbox with her. Probably a few pieces of rinky-dink junk like the kind of mail-order gadgets his sisters were always using to hang pictures, open jar lids and pry open stuck drawers.

Priority one: lay in enough food supplies to last through the rest of the winter, come hell, hurricane or high water.

Priority two: tools. Top quality stuff, because a man couldn't do a first-rate job with second-rate tools, and before he took off, he intended to do a first-rate job of making this place safe until she could find herself something better.

Then, too, if she got really hard up, there was always a market for good used power tools. If a woman was sentimental, it would beat the hell out of pawning the ancestral pearls.

Smugly, Keegan tested his muscles. He flexed his back experimentally and was satisfied with the result. "Now we'll see about taking care of Miss Maudie," he muttered, once more on top of the situation.

Maudie repaired the torn screen and then removed the hanging shutter and stored it underneath the cottage until she could replace the hinge. She was sorely tempted to replace it with one from the Hunt. The original Keegan had used solid brass hardware throughout, heavy, ornate stuff that was probably worth a small fortune now. Some of it had been stolen long before she took on the job of caretaker. The rest was tarnished to a lovely shade of green. Green or not, she might have borrowed one, but Maudie had always been conscious of the fact that whatever remained of the Hunt belonged to the Keegans. The owners of the five cottages could have afforded to buy brass if they'd wanted to, but had settled for galvanized, instead. It was cheaper and almost as practical, if not so pretty, and goodness knows, Maudie could appreciate practicality.

All the same, she had come to love the scrolled brass hinges, the ornate millwork, the hand painted Italian tiles and all the lovely little details that no one ever bothered with anymore. Of course, it wasn't practical these days, but all the same, it was a shame.

Regina. Maudie had been feeding the poor old racoon outside Hawk's Nest, where she'd first found her, too old and blind to fend for herself and in danger of starving.

"Regina, love, you're going to have to mend your ways. Your teeth might be worn down to the gum, but there's nothing wrong with your claws, is there?"

Her father had warned her that the animal might be rabid, but Maudie decided she was just old. Old, arthritic, hungry and lonely. Regina lived in a hollow in an old live oak tree that was in little better condition than she was, which probably explained why she kept trying to move into one of the cottages. Maudie tried for several minutes to lure her out, to catch a glimpse of her just to be sure she was all right, but Regina's siestas usually lasted for most of the day.

"Okay, don't let me disturb your nap." Leaving the bundle of cheese rinds and a withered apple at the base of the sprawling old oak, she crooned, "We'll make it, won't we, honey? Who needs some ring-tailed hotshot complicating our lives?"

It was nearly noon when Maudie got back to the Hunt. Back to her nest, as she had come to think of it, although since the Keegan had burst onto the scene, her nest no longer felt quite so cozy and secure.

He was waiting for her, leaning up against the pine where she had mounted her fish-cleaning table, his arms crossed over his chest. At a glance, he looked angry. At a closer glance he looked downright livid.

"Still here, I see," she greeted cordially.

"Surprise, surprise," he sneered.

Uh-oh. Keegan in a good mood was tolerable. Just barely. Keegan in a bad mood would be another thing altogether. "Is something wrong?"

"I could have taken yours, you know. The only reason I didn't was that I didn't want you on my conscience if a sudden storm came up and you got trapped over here on this floating sand pile."

Maudie blinked. "You want to run that by me again?"

"Don't play games with me, lady, unless you're into losing."

"I've never been partial to it, but I reckon I can handle it," she said pleasantly, wondering what the devil had happened since she'd told him goodbye not three hours ago. "Losing that is. Occasionally. Would you care for some lunch?"

"Shall I set the plates out again? I think you left half a strip of bacon and some crusts on yours. Afraid there's not much left on mine." If he'd actually laid back his ears and curled his lip at her, he couldn't have made his feelings any plainer.

"Keegan, are you feeling all right?" She was beginning to wonder if there was something wrong with the man besides a bad back and a nasty disposition.

"No, dammit, I'm not feeling all right, I'm feeling mad as hell!"

"Well, that's hardly my fault," Maudie reasoned. "I've been gone all morning."

She sauntered into the house, feeling his eyes boring into her backside with every step. If she'd followed her instincts, she would have made a dash for it and slammed the door shut behind her, but her father had told her once when she'd been chased up a tree by a pack of dogs, never to show fear. It only aggravated an already touchy situation.

He was right on her heels. She dropped her toolbox in the front room and shed her coat, slinging it by force of habit at the sturdy pipe-frame easel her father had made her. If she'd had a flute she would have yanked it out and started tooting up a storm on the theory that music hath charms to soothe the savage beast. Or was it breast?

Whatever.

Of course, even if she'd had a flute, she couldn't play a note. Couldn't even whistle on key, but that was neither here nor there at the moment. "Look, is there something you want to get off your chest?" she finally demanded.

"Who, me?" The wretch feigned surprise.

"No, Dolly Parton," she shot back. And then, "Of course, you. You're the one who told me not to play games, so would you kindly do me the same courtesy? I'm not into twenty questions."

"So let's make it one question," he said silkily, pinning her with those cobalt eyes of his. "Like…where'd you put it?"

"Put *what?*" she wailed. "If I've inadvertently misplaced something of yours, I assure you it was an accident. Tell me what it is and where you last saw it, and—"

"An accident. Right. You were walking by my outboard and the spark plug wire accidentally fell off. So tell me, did you hear a splash? Could it have flown overboard? Because believe me, I searched every inch of your boat and mine, and you're damned lucky I didn't rob yours to fix mine! The only thing that kept me from it was the thought of you being stranded over here without transportation in an emergency!''

Silence grew into a vacuum. And then Maudie said very quietly, "Oh."

"Oh?"

"I forgot."

"You forgot."

"Are you going to repeat everything I say?"

"I haven't decided what I'm going to do! Give me time, I'm still considering the options."

Maudie didn't like the glint in his eyes. She didn't care at all for the way he was flexing his jaw. Swallowing back her nervousness, she reached for her coat and removed the small insulated wire from her right-hand pocket where she had put it the day before and forgotten it. Out tumbled a tissue, a copper nail and the roasted peanut she had meant to give Regina. "Sorry. Since you're getting off to a late start, would you care for some lunch first?"

"No, thanks," Keegan said grittily, but at the thought of food, his stomach gave an audible rumble, and Maudie's lips twitched.

"The man may not be hungry, but the beast is," she teased, and Keegan felt his anger melt away like snow in a warm spring rain. The woman had that effect on him. Strange.

They eventually sat down to sandwiches made of cheese, sardines, coleslaw and onions, an unlikely choice, he would have thought, for a petite female with spruce green eyes and a voice as soft as an August fog.

Ah, jeez, he didn't need this. Whatever it was she did to him, he really didn't need the complication at this point in his life.

She poured milk into two red glasses—the same two he had filched the day before, he noted with no small degree of embarrassment. For several minutes they ate in silence, with Keegan vainly trying to manage the shaggy, juicy sandwich without dripping down the front of his next-to-last clean shirt. It was the same one he had used as a pillow. He made a mental note to hunt up a laundry while he was over on Hatteras. "I'd better get a move on," he said, wiping his mouth with a faded denim napkin that he suspected of once having been a section of pant leg.

No paper ones for this lady. It occurred to him that garbage disposal would be a problem on a place this size. It occurred to him that there were probably quite a few problems living in such an isolated place, cut off from civilization, with the nearest land another island only marginally better equipped.

It occurred to him that he was essentially a high-tech sort of guy. No wonder all this pioneer stuff was making him edgy. It wasn't the woman, it was the place.

Yeah, sure it is. That's why you've been walking on three legs ever since you set eyes on her!

"Any last requests?" he inquired politely, rising to carry his plate and glass to the sink. He washed them himself as a matter of course. Keegan had always prided himself on his self-sufficiency.

"Before you go, you mean? No...I can't think of any," Maudie replied as several things came instantly to mind. A hug—a nice, warm, comforting embrace. A kiss—the kind that uncurls inside you and sets off all sorts of interesting repercussions. A long, lazy evening of conversation about this and that and the meaning of it all. Foolish things she missed now and then when she was tired, or worried, or just plain lonesome.

Rich picked up the spark plug wire, tossed it once or twice in the air and then jammed it in his pants' pocket, and Maudie followed the action, her gaze lingering on his lean flank until she caught herself staring and turned to the sink.

"Yes, well . . . have a safe trip to wherever," she mumbled. "And drive carefully, you hear? Oh, and if you decide you want any of this stuff for your nieces and nephews, just write and I'll have someone crate it up and ship it north."

Keegan grinned, his eyes—eyes that had squinted at too many suns over the years—nearly lost in a bed of crinkles. "Thanks for everything, Maude."

"Maudie," she corrected. "Maude is my aunt. It was nice meeting you, Rich Keegan."

Keegan nodded. He collected his leather flight jacket on the way out and slung it across his shoulders. Closing the door behind him, he headed down to the pier. He knew damned well she was watching him through the window, and his walk lost some of its military precision and took on elements of a swagger. "Lady, I'm not done with you yet," he said softly, following the trail through the stunted maritime forest. "Not by a long shot."

Maudie, freshly scrubbed, warm and shrouded from toes to chin in flannel and chenille, was working on her spring garden layout, wondering if there wasn't an easier way to haul eelgrass up from the shore for mulch, when she heard the distant sound of a laboring outboard. For several moments she listened, her head tilted to one side, and then she jammed her pencil into her topknot and padded to the window just as the wind picked up the sound and carried it away.

Probably someone going up the creek over at Hatteras.

There was barely a glimmer of light left in the sky now, even though it wasn't all that late. Maudie had considered soaking out a side of salt mullet to fry—maybe making a pan of cornbread to go with her leftover coleslaw. Instead she had settled for a peanut butter sandwich. Cooking a real meal was too much trouble for one person.

One of the drawbacks of living alone was that almost everything was too much trouble for just one person. She'd been hungry for cornbread for weeks, but it seemed foolish to bake a whole skilletful for only herself. Regina didn't care much for cornbread. The gulls would eat it, but it was against her principles to turn healthy animals into beggars when she might not always be there to feed them.

Regina was different. She probably wouldn't have survived this long if she hadn't had a bit of help. Although sometimes Maudie wondered who needed whom the most.

She was drowsing in the spraddled wicker rocking chair when she heard the sound of a muffled thump. Naturally her first thought was of Regina. The old racoon often waddled past in her nocturnal rambles. Once she had even come right into the front room.

She heard it again. That was no racoon. Someone was out there. Had she actually heard the high whine of an outboard earlier, or had she only dreamed it? Heard it suddenly cut off, heard the sound of a boat grating along the pier, and the hollow sound of aluminum bumping aluminum?

Impossible. Her boat was fiberglassed marine plywood. Keegan's rental was aluminum, but Keegan was gone...wasn't he?

The glimmer of a flashlight bobbing up the path a few minutes later effectively blanked out any chance of seeing who her visitor was. With one hand on her shotgun, she opened the front door.

"Daddy?" she called softly.

"It's me, Keegan. Put your shotgun down, Maudie."

"How did you know?" she asked as he brushed past her, bringing with him the dark scent of leather, masculine sweat and outboard fuel. Her pulses lurching into a funny little quick-step, she repeated, "How did you know about the gun?"

"Because you're not fool enough to open your door without some kind of backup. Is it loaded this time?"

Maudie slipped the pink leg warmer she used as a gun case over barrel and shoved the empty .410 behind a stack of scrap lumber. Crossing her arms over her chest, she said, "Did you forget something? I thought by now you'd be on the other side of Oregon Inlet."

"Did I say anything about heading north?"

"Did you—?" Her jaw fell open.

Keegan's thumb came up under her chin and with gentle pressure, he lifted it, closing her mouth.

Maudie jerked her face away, feeling heat flood her face. "Your bag was gone."

"I went to a launderette. Washed, dried, folded and repacked everything. You don't happen to have an iron, do you? Nah—I guess you wouldn't. I'm not into flatirons."

"And I'm not into starch and creases."

"Bad habits are hard to break," he confided, his lean cheeks creasing in a grin.

Maudie was flustered. "Why didn't you keep on going?"

"I'm not ready yet to leave. You'll know it when I am."

The simple words were layered with meaning. Silently he dared her to push it. When she didn't, he said, "A lot of places are closed this time of year. You didn't warn me about that. I think I managed to get most everything on my lists, though. Jerry over at the marina was a big help. Said to tell you hello, by the way."

"Keegan, what are you—?"

"Rich. The guys call me Keegan. Women and family usually call me by my first name."

"I'm not one of your family and I'm not one of your women, Colonel! Oh, for goodness' sake—" She whirled away, face still flaming, and Keegan followed her. Leaving behind the cold night air with its essence of pine, cedar and salt marsh, he entered the cluttered room with its scarred and faded paneling, where fishing gear vied with painting gear for space. For a guy who had been perfectly content with the most austere quarters for more than half his life, Keegan was surprised at how welcoming the shabby old place felt.

"Good to be home again," he said, only half teasing. "Once the sun goes down, this place gets cold as a well digger's—ah, drill bit."

"Yes, well—stand over by the fire until you thaw out." Maudie tried to convince herself she wasn't glad to see him and knew it for a lie.

"Hey, you're not upset, are you? Did you think I was gone for good? That I'd leave without even saying goodbye?"

"Yes, I thought you were gone for good. I was banking on it. Did you leave something behind, is that why you're back?"

"Yeah," he said softly. "You might say that." With an abrupt about-face, he strode to the front door and returned a moment later with several shopping bags, which he set down on the kitchen table.

Maudie stared through the salt-hazed window at the blinking green light out in the channel, unwilling to be drawn into his little games. She was feeling raw and vulnerable in a way she hadn't felt in years. She had to snap out of it. There was no reason to feel this way—no reason whatsoever to allow some here-today, gone-tomorrow stranger to burrow into her life and upset her nice, orderly existence.

So she wouldn't. It was that simple. The choice was hers.

"Eggs—must have used up all yours this morning for breakfast. Milk—I got two percent, all right? Hey, they had these apples that looked real good, so I got us a dozen. And some cheese and butter and steaks and—"

"Keegan," she said grimly. "What do you think you're doing? I don't eat that much in a month."

"I'll help," he said with a grin that promptly shattered her hastily erected defenses.

He said he'd eaten something over on Hatteras, but she took down her smallest frying pan and grilled him another cheese sandwich and made a pot of coffee. The apples were small, but crisp and juicy. She ate two, saving the cores for Regina.

Over coffee Keegan told her about his raid on the hardware and lumber store, and then he told her about the inspection he'd done while she'd been on the other side of the island.

And then he told her about his plans.

"Now I'm not a builder, understand, but one of my brothers is a contractor. Can't help but pick up a few things, since that's about all Ken ever talks about. Surprising thing is, this old place is a lot sounder than it looks. Heart pine and cypress would be my guess. There's been some damage to the foundation on the southwest wing where the roof caved in—"

"And where the window blew out and the rain rotted out the floor and it fell through, taking a wall and a half down with it," she added dryly.

"Well, yeah—that, too. Thing is, I think I can shore things up enough so you'll have a safe place to stay until you can—well, that is, I suppose you have plans to, uh..."

"Keegan," Maudie said softly, placing her third apple core in Regina's saucer. "Why don't you just go home and forget about the Hunt and the island and—"

"And you?" He was sprawled in her wicker rocker, looking like a big, sleepy, well-sated lion after his grilled-cheese sandwich and two apples. Lions didn't eat apples. She did know that much. In fact, she probably knew more about lions than she did about men, which wasn't saying a whole lot.

While they sipped the coffee he had brought—a specially ground blend well outside her budget—Maudie considered all she knew and didn't know about the male species. Her father, for instance. His wife, Maudie's mother, had died the year before Ann Mary was born, and he had settled comfortably enough into grandfatherhood, baby-sitting while Maudie worked as a clerk five days a week and a waitress three nights a week during peak season, fishing a pound net and a few crab pots, doing a bit of gardening, whittling toys for the granddaughter he adored.

Two and a half years ago he met a widow from Buffalo and his hair turned black again overnight, his Indian-dark eyes took on a new sparkle and the back that had been stooping a bit more each year was suddenly ramrod straight.

Janine had done wonders for Medlin Burrus. She had done somewhat less for his daughter. Maudie had found herself a guest in her own home once the two of them had married, which was when she had started looking around for another place and found the Coronoke Island thing.

"Penny for 'em," Keegan murmured, his voice a deep, oddly comforting rumble. Sanford's voice had been—well, tenor was a kind way of putting it. Shrill was probably more accurate. Especially when he was upset, which had been most of the time after the first few months of their marriage.

"More coffee?" she asked, reaching for the pot. It was nice to relax and not feel forced to make conversation. Sanford, when he wasn't sulking, was a compulsive talker. Hospital gossip, usually personal, always malicious. It was one of the things Maudie had come to dislike about him. One of several things. But then, that was history. Unbelievably naive, she had fallen head over heels into what she thought was love with a handsome face, a suave manner and a persuasive style of seduction.

The amazing thing was that he'd married her at all. Herpes was the big scare at the time, and he had told her quite frankly that he intended to marry a virgin because monogamy was the only way to go.

She had discovered a little later that her virginity wasn't her only attraction. Sanford had grossly misunderstood her background. He'd had a friend who had inherited a fortune in beachfront property in Nags Head, and he seemed to think the fact that her family had "property" on the Outer Banks put her in the same category.

None of her father's property was beachfront. Most natives, knowing how ephemeral beachfront property really was, opted for something more secure. Ironically most of her father's safe, secure inland property had been rendered valueless by various environmental concerns. Sanford had been furious when he'd learned that about all she stood to inherit was an eighty-year-old frame house and an ever-increasing tax burden.

Men. They were not among nature's more dependable species. Fortunately, Maudie had learned early that she had a perfectly good brain, and she wasn't afraid of hard work. If she'd done nothing else in her life, she hoped she had passed on to her daughter the confidence to stand on her own two feet.

"A nickle, then?" Keegan mused.

In the wood stove, a log settled. Outside, the wind picked up. "How well did you secure your skiff? If the wind swings around to the northeast, it'll beat up against the pier unless you tied it off."

Keegan stood and reached toward her. She handed him her cup. He placed it on the table and reached out again, and feeling as if she'd just stepped aboard a runaway elevator, Maudie put her hand in his.

"Let me worry about that, hmm?"

Five

It was the middle of the following day before Maudie discovered the extent of Keegan's intentions. She was furious. The only thing that kept her from shoving him, the boatful of lumber he had towed behind his rental, the tools he had bought and his highfalutin plans—fully diagramed and annotated on her best sketch pad!—right off the edge of her island was the fact that he was favoring his back and trying not to show it.

Blast! She didn't want to feel sympathy. It got in the way of enjoying a good, rousing mad! It had been years since she had indulged in the luxury of a full-blown tantrum. By now she had built up a tremendous head of steam.

Maudie's great-aunt Etheldra had had a theory about temper. Swallow too much of it and it will claw its way out through your stomach. Better to let it escape a little at a time.

She'd had a thing about crying, too, which Maudie had also forgotten to heed. Hold back tears and you'll have more than your share of colds. One way or another, you're going to wheeze and your eyes and nose are going to turn red and start running. It's nature's way.

Maudie had no intention of crying. After she'd gone to bed the night before, having been tenderly kissed good night, she had whispered a few choice words into her pillow. For all the good it had done her.

The trouble was, you couldn't very well get mad at a man who was acting purely out of altruism. He was doing her a favor. Why else would he patch up an old relic that would pass out of his hands in less than three months?

"Keegan, tell me something. How could the Air Force afford to let you go? You *did* run the whole show single-handedly, didn't you?"

He sent her a dirty look and walked stiffly across to the wood stove. She had dragged him away from stacking the lumber he had hauled out from Hatteras the day before by pretending to need his advice on a stuck damper. It was either that or watch him sweat blood when his lower back muscles froze up again. "D'you want to finish off this coffee while you're in here so I can wash the pot?"

He muttered something and jiggled the coiled-wire damper handle in the section of stovepipe that led to the boarded-up window.

Maudie poured the reheated coffee into a mug and shoved it across the table. She washed the coffeepot, turned it down to drain, and then refilled her painting jar and spray bottle. She had woken up in the mood to paint—another lighthouse scene, this time with a stormy sky. Normally a blue-sky painter, she felt a powerful urge to try something dramatic. The stark bones of a wrecked ship, a turbulent, slate-gray sky, a raging sea crashing against the shore—something she could really get her teeth into!

While she set up her palette, Keegan examined the stovepipe and muttered under his breath. He downed the mug of coffee, washed out the mug and then began unpacking the tools he had purchased.

Maudie watched in silence over the edge of her canvas. She would have lent him her own tools if he'd bothered to ask, but of course, being Keegan, he hadn't.

"Your father worry about you being over here alone with a man?" he asked a few minutes later.

With a brush dipped in raw sienna, she slashed a horizontal stroke across the toned canvas. "I'm of age. Besides, he knows me pretty well."

He laid out his tools on the other side of the table, and Maudie closed her eyes and prayed for patience. "What does that mean?" he muttered.

"Probably just what you think it means. Rich, that's going to put a load on the generator." Brush held aloft, she gazed at the row of power tools he had so carefully laid out like a surgical nurse before an operation. All this, she marveled, for a measly little stuck damper? She could have cured the thing with one good whack in the right place, but she'd thought to lure him into tackling something that wouldn't put him in traction.

Keegan glanced at the woman, and then back at the tools. He flushed a dull shade of brick red. Power tools. Oh, hell. She had a gas stove, wood heat, a pitcher pump and her light bulbs wouldn't have done justice to a self-respecting firefly. "I knew that. They, uh, had a sale. Thought I may as well stock up."

Poor baby. Sure you did, she thought with an unexpected surge of sympathy.

"What I really need is a thin-bladed knife," he mumbled.

"Crock on the shelf in the corner."

Holding himself stiffly, he turned, reached for the jar of knives, and selected her best fileting knife. She'd just whetstoned it two days before. "Careful, it's sharp."

With a speaking look, he tested it on his thumb and then tackled her stovepipe with the tip of the blade. One good whack in the right place, she longed to say—that's all it needs. Certainly not major surgery with my best fish cleaning knife.

Biting her tongue, Maudie turned back to her canvas. It was pre-stretched and pre-primed, bottom of the line stuff. Being fairly certain she was no candidate for any artistic hall of fame, she wasn't about to spend a small fortune on handwoven linen stuff and then have to stretch, prime and gesso it herself. A great artist she wasn't; practical, she was.

Tongue between her teeth, she was just sketching the major compositional lines when the crash came. It was followed by a curse, a groan, and a billow of soot, and she dropped her brush in the water jar, sprayed a whiff of water over her palette and shoved it into a plastic bag.

Next time she'd ask him to unstick the lid on her hand lotion bottle. At least he might be able to handle that without bringing down the roof on their heads. "Did you hurt yourself?"

"Judas priest, lady, it's a wonder you haven't burned the whole island down with this jury-rigged piece of junk!"

"It does the job. Or rather, it did. Come over here to the sink and I'll wash the soot out of your eyes."

"I'll take care of my own damned eyes," he growled, sending two stools tumbling as he charged blindly across the room.

Resigned to an afternoon spent scrubbing instead of painting, Maudie surveyed the mess he had made. All right, so the stovepipe was rusty. It had needed replacing, but she had hoped that with care it would last out the season.

Operating mostly by feel, Keegan pumped himself a dishpan full of the brackish groundwater used for all except cooking and drinking. He splashed it on his face—and incidentally, his shirt, the wall behind the sink, and the floor—leaving gray puddles everywhere.

Patiently, Maudie stood in the ruins of her once-neat living quarters and waited for him to ask for help. She might have known he wouldn't, even when it was obvious that he had something in his left eye that was causing it to tear.

If Etheldra's theory held, he shouldn't get many colds this year. "Need a hand?" she offered when it looked as if he'd go blind before asking for help.

"I can get it."

"Fine," she said, and turned to start gathering up the sections of ruined stovepipe. Sparks flew from the hole at the back of the stove, and calmly, she covered it with a battered aluminum biscuit pan and closed the bottom door tightly to cut off the draft.

Using pliers to keep from burning her hands, she had taken the first two sections to the front door and laid them outside on bare sand when Keegan said, "Uh, Maudie, d'you think you could take a look at my eye? Must've caught a piece of flak."

"Rust, probably. Here, come over to the window where I can see it."

Given a grain of common sense, Maudie would have kept her hands in her pockets. That kiss should have tipped her off that she was allergic to big, raw-boned, chauvinistic, by-the-book throwbacks like Richmond Keegan, Col., USAF, retired.

But for the first time in more than twenty years, her common sense failed her, and Maudie reached up with both hands just as Keegan leaned over.

She could have picked up a live wire with less damage. The minute she felt the warm, leather-on-granite texture of him, she stiffened. How long had it been since she'd held a man's face between her hands? How long since she'd felt the lightning jolt of sheer sexual awareness streak through her body?

"My left eye," he whispered, his voice sounding oddly hollow. She saw his lips move, and it dawned on her that he had spoken. Slowly she dragged her gaze away from his mouth, past his rather large nose, which now looked as if he'd been out in the sun too long, to his eyes, which were inflamed and brimming with tears.

"Hold still." Inhaling deeply, she slipped her right hand up to his forehead and moved her thumb to his eyelid. "Don't blink."

He blinked furiously. Tears spilled over to trickle down the craggy planes of his face. "Ah, jeez," he groaned, and his hands closed over her shoulders, as if to steady them both.

"Ah-*ha!*" Maudie exclaimed softly. With a forefinger, she touched his left cheek and then showed him the fleck of rust that had been flushed from his eye by the tears. "Nature's cure."

Keegan blinked several times experimentally. "I think that's got it."

He tried to straighten up, and three things happened. He swore. Maudie said "Oh, no," and the last section of stovepipe fell to the floor with a tinny crash.

* * *

Two days later, Maudie was fit to be tied. Keegan had insisted on staying out of her way, which meant that she'd had to clean up her front room and move the daybed, the door and the big chair out there, leaving her with nowhere to relax. And then suffer his dire predictions on how long it would take for the worn-out two-by-fours to collapse, bringing the whole shaky structure down on his head.

"I did offer you Ann Mary's room," she'd reminded him.

"With a wet bed and a single boarded-up window? No, thanks."

"I can dry the mattress if you'll help me drag it out into the sunshine. I can spread a tarp where it'll catch the afternoon sun and by night it'll be aired and dry."

Keegan watched as a slant of sunshine spilling in from the west window set rainbows to dancing on her head. Her hair was light brown, definitely not dark blond. Funny, he'd never before realized how different the two shades were.

"On second thought, it probably wouldn't do your back any good. Never mind, I can manage alone. There's a dolly in the boat house."

That irked him. Independent women were one thing, but did she have to make him feel like a basket case? "Don't go to any trouble on my account," he muttered ungraciously. "I never sleep in a room without a window." He didn't bother to add that the dark, corridor-like room was too much like solitary confinement for a man who had experienced the real thing.

So she let it drop. As easy as that. He wondered briefly if she would be as agreeable if he asked to share her bed.

Down, boy. She's not your type. You like 'em tall and torrid, remember? Her legs are too short, her boobs are

*too big and her beam too broad. Besides, a woman all that
placid would probably fall asleep halfway between the ap-
petizer and the entrée.*

So Keegan had moved out into the front room, and
Maudie had gone on treating him like a stray footstool that
no one ever used. Unneeded. Unwanted. In the way. And
he alternately simmered and brooded. Why couldn't she
just come right out and tell him to get the hell off her island? She'd been quick enough on the trigger that first day.
What did it take to get a rise out of a woman like Maudie
Winters?

Keegan told himself he should've got out while getting
was good, aching back and all. But he'd hung around, and
now, whether or not she would admit it, the air between
them was getting more explosive by the minute.

And, dammit, if she wouldn't light the fuse, then he was
going to have to, because every time he blew his cool and
snapped at her, and she retaliated with that unflappable
smile of hers, he ended up feeling mean as two tomcats in
a washing machine, which only made things worse.

She wanted him gone. No matter how polite she was, she
wanted him out of here. The crazy part was that his internal radar kept telling him she was interested in him as a
man. Which was pretty heady stuff, because he was sure as
hell interested in her as a woman. Strictly in a physical
sense, of course. On a temporary basis. Because she really
wasn't his type.

"What are you, a master of disguise?" he'd asked her
just that morning. She'd been on her way over to Hatteras
to buy stovepipe. "Um, make that a mistress. Sorry.
Didn't mean to offend your feminist sensibilities."

Maudie had smiled that butter-wouldn't-melt smile of
hers and Keegan had felt the pressure start to rise again. "I
don't think there's any way you can win on that one,"

she'd drawled. "I'm not quite sure what you mean, though."

With a thoroughness that was meant to be insulting, Keegan had let his gaze roam her small but exceedingly adequate topography in a way good manners would ordinarily preclude. "A miniature Amazon. Sort of a—whatchamacallit? Oxymoron? Like a superette?"

If she'd decked him, he wouldn't have blamed her, but instead, she refused to take offense. It *had* to be deliberate! No woman could accidentally drive a man around the bend without even working up a sweat. He was no green kid. He'd cut his teeth on women who would make Maudie Winters look like Betty Crocker's maiden aunt.

Keegan told himself he was a reasonable guy. He liked women, children, animals, and occasionally he even went to church. He wasn't pushing any particular agenda, he was just marking time, getting his head together before he decided what he wanted to do with the rest of his life.

So what the hell was there not to like about him?

Because she didn't. Like him, that was. Without raising her voice, without so much as a crack in that soft, Southern hospitality shtick, she managed to make it painfully clear that she wanted his tail out of there the minute he could get it in gear.

Sitting in a patch of sunshine that helped alleviate the damp chill of the old ruin, Keegan tried once more to sort it all out. Why she didn't like him, and why the hell he cared? He'd never claimed to be God's gift to women, but jeez, he couldn't be all *that* bad! He bathed regularly. He shaved every morning. He changed his socks and underwear every day. That alone was no small thing, considering that all he had to work with was a wood stove, a kettle and a thirty-gallon galvanized washtub. His tailor-mades would never be the same.

Did she even care that he was staying on just to make things better for her? Hell, no, she didn't care! She looked down that stubby little nose of hers as if he was something she'd found belly-up on her beach at the end of a long, hot day.

And she smiled!

Raking his chair back, Keegan got to his feet and started to pace, fists rammed into the pockets of his rumpled trousers. It was screwy. The whole thing was just plain screwy! His ego hadn't taken such a beating since Alice had written that she'd seen a lawyer about starting divorce proceedings and would appreciate it very much if he would cooperate.

Keegan knew his own worth. For one thing, he was a damned good pilot. He'd been flying since he was sixteen. Actually, since he was eleven, but that was strictly off the record. He'd seen action in the Gulf War and a few so-called police actions and been decorated more times than he could remember. In his twenties, he'd been a hot-stick pilot. In his thirties, he'd been an ace. At forty-two, his reflexes and cardiovascular, while slightly below his personal peak, were still better than most non-flying types half his age. Even if his vision wasn't.

So why the hell should he need approval from some middle-aged female Robinson Crusoe?

What he needed was something to get his mind ticking over again. Such as an immediate goal. A project. Something to keep him occupied until he felt right about clearing out and leaving her to her fate.

Meanwhile, he could at least check out the chimney and see if she couldn't do better than poke a stovepipe through a boarded-up window. Had that even occurred to her?

The sun was shining. Back home there was probably two feet of snow on the ground. The kids would be skiing and making snowmen. Ken would be worrying about the delay in housing starts, and Babe would be worrying about Benji's bronchitis. Edie would be bribing her pair to shovel off the driveway so she could get to the shelter with a load of blankets. She'd strip her family's beds if she thought some poor down-on-his-luck devil needed it.

On Coronoke, the temperature at 1422 hours was fifty-five and falling. Keegan shed his shirts, and as an afterthought, his pants. Skivvies were a lot easier to launder. At least he didn't have to worry about the creases.

He was flat on his back, head in a massive fireplace, when he heard the guttering whine of her outboard. He had checked out the four standing chimneys and this one just might—he inched in a little deeper, his eyes narrowed against falling debris—just *might* possibly be sound.

A few minutes later, he was sure of it. There wasn't one damned thing wrong with this big mama—she was sound as the day she'd been built. He'd checked from the roof first of all, using a flashlight and the ladder he'd found around on the far side. The mortar was solid enough so that even on the top, where weathering was a problem, he couldn't chip it out with a knife. Next thing he would do was to—

"Keegan, what in the world do you think you're doing?"

Oh, hell. In his excitement, he'd forgotten that he wasn't exactly dressed for receiving.

Maudie stared disbelievingly down at the filthy figure sprawled out on the hearth in the fireplace of what had once been the main gathering room of the Hunt, according to her father.

"Careful," she cautioned, but her mind was not on the injury he might do himself, nor even on whatever absurd reason he might have dreamed up for poking around in this part of the Hunt in the first place. Dear heavenly days, the man was built like a—like a *man!*

Maudie couldn't remember when she'd felt so acutely aware of her own situation. Her own deprivation. It had never particularly bothered her before, probably because she'd been working her tail off for years to support her family. Which wasn't to say she didn't suffer sometimes from a loneliness that was so bone deep she almost forgot it was there. But this wasn't loneliness, this was pure, un-adulterated *lust!*

"You're back, huh?"

"I'm back. Do you mind telling me what you think you're doing?"

"Trying to find an outlet for your stove. Don't tell me that window rig you were using ever passed any safety in-spection."

He was sitting on the hearth in his briefs and T-shirt, one knee drawn up and an arm slung carelessly across it as he leaned back on the other one. He was filthy. Ridiculously, magnificently, sexily, filthy!

"In case it escaped your notice, Colonel, civilization is stretched pretty thin by the time it gets out this far. Coronoke doesn't have fire inspections. Mainly because it doesn't have a fire department. Mainly because if it did, I'd be it, and I'm busy enough as it is."

She kept her gaze pinned to his eyes, determined not to look below his Adam's apple, but it didn't help. She had excellent peripheral vision.

"Got the pipe?"

"Yes, I got the pipe."

"Good. Because I've got news for you. There's not a thing wrong with this chimney. It's as sound as the day it was built. Evidently it hasn't been used much since the last time it was cleaned, so that—"

"Which was about 1958, if I'm not mistaken."

"—so that if we can move the stove into this room we can...we can, uh..."

Maudie waited for him to tell her how comfortable they would be with the stove in one wing of the house and her living quarters in the other. Evidently he'd done enough exploring so that he'd completely lost sight of how far he had come from the main portion, where she had chosen to take up residence.

"Yeah," he mumbled. "Right."

She could almost feel sorry for him. It couldn't be easy for a man like Rich Keegan, a man completely unused to having his authority questioned, to admit he had made a mistake. "Are you hungry?" she asked gently. "You'll probably want to get cleaned up first."

Keegan looked down at his once white skivvies. Slow heat suffused his features and he swore under his breath. "Look, I'm sorry. I guess I just got carried away."

Maudie made an effort to seem fascinated by the ruined grandeur of cherry paneling with eight-inch crown molding and warped and water-blackened oak parquet floors. One section of the roof had been damaged during a recent hurricane, allowing water to flood into the wing whenever it rained.

"Why don't you go heat some water on the gas stove while I unload the stovepipe, and then—"

"I'll do that," he said gruffly, coming to his feet in one lithe movement that belied his body's nearly forty-two years of hard usage.

She backed away, her face as red as his, and Keegan watched as she turned and fled, wondering what was going on under that topknot of pale brown silk. Surely she wasn't embarrassed at catching a man in his underwear?

Hell, she'd seen men wearing less than this on the beach if she'd grown up down here—probably a hell of a lot less.

Telling himself she couldn't have been turned on by the sight of his hairy legs—although he was more than a little turned on by the possibility that she *had* been—he followed the sandy trail around to the landward side of the Hunt. On the way he spotted the mangy old racoon he'd seen snooping around once or twice, looking for a handout.

He'd tossed out a few scraps just that morning, trying to lure the poor old critter closer, but it had waddled off without even investigating. He had felt oddly rejected.

Just before he reached the front door, Keegan remembered the other surprise he had for her. He hoped this one would turn out better than the last one had.

Keegan was no stickler, but—okay, so maybe he was. The thing was, those frying pans of hers had been driving him nuts ever since he'd first got a look at their condition. Nobody—not even sweet, Southern-talking little ladies with green eyes and skin like old ivory, should be allowed to mistreat good equipment that way.

It had taken him practically all morning, using sand, detergent and elbow grease, and while his fingernails might never be clean again, those cast-iron frying pans of hers would pass a white glove inspection with flying colors!

He was grinning expectantly when he shoved open the front door. "Maudie?" he called out softly.

No answer. Gathering up a set of clean, line-dried skivvies, a shirt and his cleanest pair of service pants, he headed for the bathroom, trying to suppress a big grin.

Maybe she hadn't noticed them yet. He shot a look through the kitchen door. She was sitting at the table, the middle-size pan in her lap. She was staring at it as if . . .

"Maudie? Is something wrong?" Keegan's grin faded slowly. A heaviness settled on his stomach. "Maudie?"

Oh, hell, she was crying. He tossed his clean clothes onto a stool and took a couple of uncertain steps in her direction. "Hey, sweetheart, it's not that big a deal, honest. They just needed a good scrubbing, okay? And I didn't have anything particularly pressing to do, so I—uh..."

Jeez, she looked as if someone had jerked the legs out from under her. Hadn't anyone ever done anything nice for her before?

Keegan took two more steps, his arms outstretched, and then the instinct called situation awareness, one that had been fine-tuned on a battlefield on the other side of the world, kicked in. "You aren't happy, right?"

"Oh, no—that is, I—" She swallowed hard, and he could have sworn her eyes were brimming over, but in a dark paneled room with a total of sixty-five watts to see by, he couldn't be certain.

And then she smiled up at him. A single tear caught the glimmer of light, and suddenly, soot and all, Keegan was beside her, drawing her up into his arms.

"There, there, sugar, I didn't mean to make you cry. Ah, poor baby—" His lips were buried in her hair, and it still smelled like clover, and the feel of her body, small, soft in some places, firm in others, was doing things to him that he hadn't counted on—things he was in no condition to follow through on at the moment. "Look, you don't have to thank me. I just wanted to do something for you in appreciation for all you've done for me. I mean, the door, the meals, putting up with me this way. I mean, it can't be easy, having a strange man drop in on you out of the blue. I never meant—"

"Rich, you don't—"

"—to hang around, you know. I never meant to cause you any trouble, but—"

"—don't understand, I'm not crying because—"

"I know, sweet pea, you don't have to say it. It was the least I could do. Look, there's things a woman shouldn't be expected to tackle, and those frying pans of yours had just about reached the place where—"

"—because you ruined my pans, I'm crying because—"

"—they were past redempti—" Keegan froze. Silence ticked away like a bomb. And then, "You wanna run that by me again?"

Maudie did, and she didn't, and she did. He was filthy, and she was clean. He was holding her, and all in the world she wanted to do right now was wrap her arms around his waist and bury her face in his chest and hang on for the next few years.

He had tried to do something kind for her. It wasn't his fault that what he had done had broken her heart. When a woman has spent years getting a pan seasoned just right, so that it never even has to be rinsed out, and when someone ruins it in a matter of minutes—

But when that someone was a man who didn't know any better, a big, airplane-flying man who knew all about high-tech things she probably couldn't even pronounce, and when he was doing it not because the law said he had to, or because he felt obligated, but because he simply wanted to be, well, to be *nice* to her....

"Oh, Lordy," she blubbered, smearing his soot with her tears as she rubbed her face against his rock-hard, ever-so-comforting chest.

She cried a long time. A lot longer than three frying pan's worth, the way Keegan figured it. The way he figured it, she probably had a lot of tears stored up inside, just waiting for a trigger to set them off. And if he could provide her with that trigger, then it wasn't a complete loss, was it? Because a person needed to cry now and then. Hell, he'd done his share of it when he hadn't known from moment to moment whether or not he would ever see the light of day again, much less his family.

"I'll buy you a new frying pan," he promised. "I'll buy you a dozen pans!" He placed a lingering kiss on her forehead. "Cry, sweetheart, you go ahead and cry," he murmured, feeling dangerously close to shedding a few tears himself. Better to bawl his eyes out than to do what he wanted to do more than he'd wanted anything in a long, long time.

Which was to take her into that bedroom and figure out a way to make love to her all night long without winding up in traction for the foreseeable future.

Six

The chimney debacle was bad enough, but the frying pan business just about did him in. Keegan couldn't remember when he'd felt like such a first-class jackass. Nor when he'd wanted so much to appear otherwise in a woman's eyes.

He reasoned that it was because he wasn't on his own turf, but when a man's turf has been a moving target for half his lifetime, that didn't make much sense.

It wasn't just the chimney—not thinking things through and winding up looking like a fool. Just as it wasn't those precious frying pans of hers that had been handed down from some old Aunt Somebody-or-other who'd spent years perfecting them, only to have him ruin them in one short morning.

It was more... and it was less. And it was the more that scared the hell out of him, because it didn't make sense. Sure, she was easy to get along with after their initial flap.

She was easy to look at, too, even if she was short-legged and broad in the beam. In fact, she was sexier in her generic brand blue jeans and paint-stained flannel shirts than a lot of women were in skintight satin and lace. The trouble was, his libido wasn't the only thing getting turned on by the unflappable Ms. Winters. If that had been all, he might not have worried.

It had been almost a week since Keegan had come to the island to check out a loose end for his family. He was still here. Being methodical by nature, he had analyzed the situation and come up with the only possible rational cause.

Somebody or *something* had cast a spell over him. And while some might call the island picturesque—it was sure as hell off the beaten track!—Coronoke was no Camelot. Roughly forty acres, give or take a few, of sand, marsh and trees, with an appropriate allotment of livestock, including mosquitoes. So far he had inventoried one mangy old racoon, three field mice, a couple dozen big crows, some pelicans and half a hundred or so gulls, various sizes and wing patterns.

Other than that, there were the five cottages that provided Maudie with her livelihood, a two-plank pier, a so-called boat house roughly the size of a two-hole privy that was reputed to hold a spare outboard, a dolly and a couple of batteries.

And the Hunt. Keegan's Hunt. Keegan's Dump, more like.

Hell, he'd even gone so far as to speculate on the possibilities for restoring the place until he'd come back down to earth and remembered the location.

Magical? Spellbinding?

Oh, hell, no! About all you could say for Coronoke was that it didn't have too much of a traffic problem. A painter might like it. A writer or a composer might enjoy the privacy, but Keegan was none of the above. He was a reluctant part of the peace dividend, a would-be lifer who'd been encouraged for medical reasons to eject from the force prematurely. He was also a hardheaded realist, a product of twenty-one years of a tough discipline, and he was damn well planning on spending his twilight years somewhere where he didn't have to cope with generators, septic tanks, wood stoves and rusty stovepipes.

Not to mention wells that produced water that was only slightly less briny than the Pamlico Sound.

On the other hand, it was hardly the most primitive place he'd ever stayed. The dump where he'd been held captive when he wasn't being trundled around from one prime target area to another, had been the pits. Quite literally. But from what he'd seen so far, this place ran a close second. With a damp wind blowing in off the water, it never quite warmed up, even when the temperature approached sixty before the sun took another dive.

Besides which, Keegan missed keeping up with the news, sweating out the latest international crisis, swearing at the latest political blunder. There wasn't a single newsstand within a hundred miles, and he couldn't even tune in to C-spann.

He glanced automatically at the watch that had cost him a month's pay and his eyes widened. Frowning, he shook his wrist and peered closer.

It had stopped. His top of the line, precision-engineered chronometer had stopped working approximately thirteen and three-quarter hours ago and he *hadn't even noticed!*

Keegan shook his head in amazement. Absently he reached for another oyster and stroked the rough surface with his thumb as he considered the fact that the world had evidently been rolling along tolerably well without his even being aware of it.

Yeah-h-h...and come to think of it, his shoulders didn't start tightening up every time he saw some Pentagon spokesman come on camera. Matter of fact, he had an idea his blood pressure was lower than it had been in some time, too. He didn't feel that old tightening sensation in his neck.

As for his back, so long as he didn't throw too much torque onto it too quickly, it didn't seem inclined to give him any more grief.

"Well, lawdy, Miss Maudie," he marveled softly, a grin breaking over his craggy face like dawn on a rocky coast. Stretching his legs out before him, he leaned back on the crude stool and pressed his back against the sun-warmed shingles. Unlikely as it was, it seemed that he had succeeded in finding something on this microcosmic continent that he wasn't even aware he'd been looking for. Something he had never found anywhere else in the world. Not in his parents' noisy home. Not in his ex-wife's fancy, all-white apartment. Certainly not in any BOQ on any base where he'd ever been stationed.

Absently thumbing the oyster knife in his right hand, Keegan applied it to the plump bivalve in his left. Maudie had taken them up that morning before he'd realized what she was doing. He had insisted on opening them. Her poor little hands were scarred enough as it was.

Frowning, he waved away a mosquito with the blade of the sharp instrument. Maudie's hands...

Keegan had known plenty of women who worked with their hands. Pilots, mechanics—one of the best gunnery officers he'd ever known was female right down to the hot pink toenails inside her combat boots.

So why the devil should Maudie's callused little hands affect him the way they did? As far as size went, they were pretty well scaled to her fuselage. Shapely, too, with long, tapering fingers, the nails invariably clean and well trimmed, even if there were usually traces of paint ingrained in her skin—not to mention the odd cut. They were unusually graceful, too. He got a kick out of watching them in action.

But there was sure as hell nothing soft about them, so why was it that the touch of those particular hands on his face had the power to send him into orbit quicker than the pampered palms of a hundred other women? The mere thought of those magic hands of hers on his body was enough to—

A film of sweat cooled his skin. Magic, hell! Enough with this Camelot crap! Okay, so the woman had nice hands, and, occasionally, she happened to use them when she talked. So did his old poker-playing buddy, Hog Hamilton. So did every two-bit politician who'd ever climbed up on a soapbox.

But Maudie's hands were different. Keegan's lips twitched in a one-sided smile as he thought about the woman who was so placid she seldom raised an eyebrow, much less her voice. Those hands of hers were a sure barometer, whether she knew it or not. He rather suspected she didn't. Watching them was like watching a Thunderbolt and a JU-87 rolling in and out of the barrel, juggling for position. Like watching the elegant mating dance of a pair of butterflies. Like watching the fluid motion of a—

"Ready for the stew?"

His arms flailed for balance, and Maudie lunged to rescue the pan that held three oysters and a lot of crumbled shell.

"Hey, uh, not quite. Give me five more minutes."

He'd already had thirty-five. Maudie hoped her growling stomach wouldn't give away her impatience. She had borrowed two well-seasoned frying pans from Janine, who preferred nonstick electric ones, and the cornbread was already baking in one of them.

"Five minutes," she said, hoping he would still have all his fingers left. Opening oysters was easy when one knew just where to pry. A novice could take forever and ruin the broth with grit and shell. Maudie figured salvaging Keegan's ego was worth a little extra roughage in her stew.

An hour and twenty minutes later, they sat down to cold cornbread, a salad that wasn't quite as crisp as it should have been, and bowls full of plump oysters floating in a buttery, opalescent broth that had been strained three times and was still gritty.

"Where's the milk?"

"There's some in the refrigerator. I thought you wanted coffee."

"I mean—well, what's this thin gray stuff?" He gestured with his spoon.

Maudie's chin lifted a fraction of an inch. "This thin gray stuff, as you call it, is oyster stew."

"If we're low on milk, you should have told me. I could have run over to Hatteras."

"We're not low on milk. There's nearly a quart of two percent left. Do you want molasses or butter or both on your cornbread?"

"This stuff's white." He examined the crusty slab of cornbread. "Are we out of eggs, too?"

Calmly, Maudie reached for the pitcher of molasses. "Seven left in the carton last time I looked."

"Then why didn't you use a few in the bread?"

"I used one. One's all it takes." She proceeded to eat, leaving Keegan to grumble about his food. She had learned right off that he was incredibly provincial for a man who had traveled to more parts of the world than she could spell.

Suspiciously, he examined one of the oysters, its skirts ruffled from being sizzled in butter. "Not even any tomatoes?"

With a sigh, she laid down her spoon. "Keegan, we're not in New England, in case it escaped your notice. Neither are we in Manhattan. Here on the Outer Banks, we make oyster stew with oysters and oyster juice. We season it with butter and black pepper, and if you don't like it, dump catsup on it. Or pour milk in it. Or crumble your cornbread in it. Or feed it to Regina, I don't care."

She commenced eating again, and Rich, flushing a dull red and hearing in his imagination both his mother and his grandmother chiding him for discussing his food while he was a guest at the table, followed suit. After a while, he had to admit that it wasn't all that bad. In fact, it was really pretty good. He didn't know that much about cornbread, as his family tended to prefer other types of bread, but he'd always thought it was supposed to be yellow. And crumbly.

"Regina?" he repeated after several minutes had passed with only the wail of the wind and the clink of stainless steel on china to be heard.

Maudie told him who Regina was. "I save scraps for her. She's not much of a hunter anymore."

She saved scraps for a racoon. Not for herself, Keegan thought. No wonder the old fleabag hadn't been interested in his attempts to feed her. And here he'd been feeling rejected!

Keegan shrugged and pried another slice of cornbread from the crusty black iron skillet.

* * *

Maudie was painting the next afternoon when Keegan poked his head through the door to announce he was going to run over to Hatteras to see if he could find a larger crowbar.

"Tide's low."

"So?"

"Shoals." She gilded the tip of a gull's wing with cadmium yellow and stepped back to examine the effect. Somehow her stormy seascape had mellowed considerably since she had first conceived it.

"So I'll avoid them. You need anything at the store?"

"Maybe I'd better run you over," she murmured, intent on matching the yellow to a streak of backlit cloud.

Keegan planted his fists on his narrow hips and glared at her. "What is it, you think I don't have sense enough not to run aground? For your information, Mrs. Winters, I happen to have navigated a—"

"Sorry. Did I give that impression? My mind's on something else," she murmured, and went right on painting. She was beginning to wonder if he had started life in the defensive mode. *Did I give you the impression I couldn't change my own diapers, Mother? I'll have you know I was dressing myself before I was even born!*

Ann Mary had been independent as a toddler, too, but Maudie had never seen the likes of Rich Keegan. Maybe it had to do with his back. For a strong man to have to admit to a weakness couldn't be easy. Sanford had been riddled with weaknesses that she hadn't discovered until too late, only he'd never admitted a single one of them. It had probably been the knowledge of his own hidden inadequacies that had made him . . . mean. Manipulative. Abusive.

Heaven help his patients if they ever discovered that Dr. Winters wasn't God, Maudie thought with a sad little smile.

Ten minutes later she dropped her brush in water and gave her palette one last whiff of water before slipping it into a plastic bag. One thing about living in a humid climate—acrylics were a lot easier to handle.

She gave him half an hour before heading for the pier. If he'd made it across, he would never know she had checked up on him. If he hadn't . . .

Well, a woman could do only so much to protect a man's ego.

His feet blue and his temper red hot, Keegan tried to shove his rented boat off the shoal, but the current was against him. The damned water was leaking out of the sound faster than he could wade! He'd wasted valuable time trying to back her off with the motor, and only as a last resort had he shed his shoes and socks, rolled up his pant legs and hopped overboard.

With the wind blowing his curses back in his face, he didn't hear Maudie's outboard until she idled up to the edge of the shoal. "Need a tow?" she called out.

"No, lady, I need some water!"

"Sorry. Fresh out. I thought maybe your outboard gave out on you."

He bared his teeth in a parody of a smile, his eyes remaining untouched. "No, you didn't. You waited until you knew I'd rammed her onto a shoal and then you hightailed it out here to tell me you told me so. Well, go to it, lady! Have fun. You've earned gloating pr'vileges."

While talking, he had slogged through thigh-deep water to grab the gun'l of her homemade skiff. With his face so close he could see the shards of gold fracturing the green of her irises, see the sunlit tips of her dark brown lashes, he ducked his head and swore.

"Hey, look, I'm sorry, all right? I was way out of line."

"Out of water would be more like it," Maudie said gently. "It gets real tricky sometimes, trying to gauge the flow this close to the inlet. Depending on the way the wind's blowing, sometimes the water rushes out of there so fast it will make your head swim."

"Or run aground trying," he said dryly, and she smiled.

Keegan was still trying to analyze the mysterious power of a woman's smile when it faded, and she said, "You're freezing! Rich, get in here and—no, wait—let's get your shoes and socks first. Here, you hold her off and I'll see if I can—"

Working together, they managed to get an anchor out on Keegan's rental. Keegan transferred the gas can and the outboard, and in a gesture that he recognized as purely a sop to his manhood, Maudie indicated that he was to take the controls of her boat.

He shook his head. "I'd sooner be certain I'm going to make shore in the near future, thanks."

Her expressive hands signaled "So be it," and they both grinned.

By the time they reached the pier, he was shaking hard. By the time they reached the Hunt, he was swearing with every step, because with every muscle in his body rigid with cold, there was no way he was going to be able to spare his back.

Dammit, he'd had plans for that back! Maybe not tonight. Maybe not even tomorrow night, but soon. At least *once* before he left this forsaken dump, and if he got real lucky, maybe even more than once. Somewhere in the shady recesses of his mind, Keegan had been counting on making a few memories he could pull out and warm him-

self by in years to come. Memories of a handful of unforgettable days and some even more unforgettable nights
spent with a calm, capable woman with the face and disposition of a saint and a body that would tempt one.

So much for tall and torrid.

Sometime after midnight the temperature bottomed out
at just above freezing. Keegan, coiled into an angular fe-
tal position for warmth, thought longingly of the pair of
thick woolen socks stashed with the rest of his gear on the
other side of the room. He'd gone to bed well fortified with
a medicinal dose of Maudie's brandy, and a second one
just in case the first one didn't do the trick. Maudie had
suggested that he sleep in his clothes.

"Thanks, but I could never sleep in anything that
binds." He slept with a night-light, which was bad enough.
Damned if he was going to regress to wearing jammies to
bed!

"Well, socks, then. At least put on a pair of socks and
wear this stocking cap." She held out a misshapen cro-
cheted thing in six shades of pink, with a pompom on the
top. "Great-Aunt Etheldra's graduation gift."

He'd laughed. So had she. And then he had gone to bed
in his skivvies, bare-footed and bare-headed.

She had insisted on layering his bed with another quilt,
and Keegan had put up only token resistance. "On top of
the seven already there? What are you trying to do, press
me for your memory book?"

She'd laughed again, and he thought she might even
have blushed, but he couldn't be sure. Earlier, they had
both had another bowl of the reheated chowder and Keegan had downed a mug of steaming coffee laced with still
more brandy before crawling under the layered covers.
Maudie had apologized for not firing the stove up to red

hot, explaining that under the circumstances, she couldn't afford to take chances with fire.

Keegan had understood. Had even praised her sensibility. And while he didn't exactly enjoy going to bed with the chickens, it was either that or share her space, pretending to read while he considered the possibilities of getting into her pants.

So now he'd had his eight hours. It was nowhere near morning, he was cold, wide awake and horny as a toad. A miserable combination. An impossible combination, he would have thought, but where Maudie Winters was concerned, Keegan was beginning to think nothing was impossible.

The woman was a witch. As for those hands of hers, they were probably magic wands in disguise.

Yeah, right. And you want to get involved with that? Man, you should have got out on a section eight instead of a straight medical!

His hurricane candle had long since guttered out, leaving the room in Stygian darkness. After roughly a quarter of an hour, Keegan decided that if he couldn't have the woman, at least he could have warm feet. Swaddled from neck to knees in a quilt, he made it almost halfway across the room before running into something cold, hard and lethal.

Swearing, he grabbed his injured toe and waited for the roof to fall. It didn't. Something clattered to the floor and a door creaked. "Rich? Is that you?"

"No, sweetheart, it's the damned tooth fairy!"

"Let me see." She switched on a tarnished brass lamp, and he heard the old generator kick in. Before he could stop her, she was on her knees at his feet—a relative position he might have given a passing thought to, but hardly in this context. "I should have remembered to—" She touched the joint that had connected with the base of her heavy pipe easel and made a clucking sound of sympathy. "I'm sorry. I should've replaced your candle. You were right, it's dangerous to go barging around in strange places in the dark."

Which was the excuse he had given her for using one in the first place.

"Wait right here and let me get something to put on it to help the bruising."

He hadn't exactly planned on running a marathon across the island. Her warm little hands closed over his big bony feet and she said, "Did you know your feet were freezing?"

Keegan closed his eyes and prayed for patience. By the time she returned with a ball of cotton and a small bottle, he was sitting on the edge of the daybed, considerably warmer. In some areas, at least.

"It's only turp, but it's artist quality. Can't do any harm, and Great-Aunt Etheldra always swore by it for bruises."

It wasn't the turpentine that scalded him, it was her hands on his naked foot. "Do you have any idea what you're doing to me?" he ground out. Judas priest, if she couldn't tell by looking at him, her precious Ann Mary must have been ordered out of a catalog! His briefs didn't leave a whole lot of room for modesty.

"By not replacing your candle, you mean? I've already apologized for that."

Keegan reached down and lifted her so that she stood between his thighs. "No, lady, not by leaving me with a two-inch stub of a candle. Not by threatening me with your shotgun. Not even by booby-trapping a stovepipe."

"Richmond," she began, her hands making small, agitated little movements at her sides.

He didn't want to hear whatever she was going to say. "Don't tell me you don't know what I'm talking about, lady, because I'm not buying it."

"Rich, listen to me—it's late, and s-sometimes late at night, a person can sort of im-imagine things, and—"

"Are you imagining what would happen if I kissed you again? I am."

"You'll catch cold. You don't have on near enough clothes." Her voice was tremulous, and Keegan had an idea it wasn't on account of the temperature. His own had just shot up into the tropics.

"More than enough, believe me. Relax," he growled. "I'm not going to do anything you don't want me to." His voice was a dark velvet promise, and even as he spoke, his hands on her shoulders were drawing her closer. He was sitting. She was standing. The height of the daybed positioned his face so that he could breathe in the warm fragrance of her breasts as he gave in to the urge to kiss the soft swell of flesh visible in the neckline of a rumpled flannel gown.

Maudie let her head fall back against the exquisite pain of desire. Fierce, urgent, honey-sweet desire. It had been years since she had felt anything even faintly like this—no, never like this. Never this strong. Never this wild compulsion to throw away all caution and follow her instincts, knowing full well it could only lead to heartache.

"Give me your mouth, Maudie," Keegan whispered.

And she did. Helplessly, knowing she was probably making the second biggest mistake of her life, she lowered her face just as he lifted his, and then he took her on his lap and turned her in his arms so that they were equal partners in all that followed.

He devoured her, and she devoured him right back. Like a starving woman, she couldn't get enough of him—of his strength, of his taste, of the clean, masculine scent of him.

Tomorrow, she told herself as reality telescoped to a blindingly brilliant moment of time, she would remind herself of all the reasons why she couldn't allow herself to become involved with a flyaway man like Rich Keegan, but for tonight she wasn't going to think at all.

Seven

Keegan breathed deeply. His nostrils flared, as if he couldn't absorb enough of her with his hands and his eyes and the length of his body. Currents and undercurrents flowed around them, far swifter than those that had driven him hard onto a shoal earlier.

Swifter, and no less dangerous, he reminded himself in one last fleeting moment of wariness.

"This is crazy," she murmured. "I don't even like muscle-headed macho types with prehistoric attitudes toward women."

He sucked her earlobe into his mouth and nipped gently. "Yeah. Mmm . . . crazy. Short women with Napoleon complexes don't turn me on, either." He did something to her that made her gasp.

"Rich, I'm nervous," Maudie whispered against his throat. The movement of her lips on his sensitive flesh raised chill bumps along his flank. He could feel her hands fluttering over his back, setting up still more currents and crosscurrents.

"Me, too," he admitted with a whimsical grin that was at odds with the dark intensity of his eyes.

"Men don't—" she began, her arms reached up around his neck, her fingertips feathering the edges of his shaggy GI.

"Men do. I want your mouth, Maudie. I want a lot more than that, but I promise I won't take anything you don't give freely."

While his hands moved over her delicate rib cage, flirting with the softness of her surprisingly full breasts, his mouth brushed back and forth, dragging against the heated moisture of her lips. With the tip of his tongue, he teased the edges of her teeth, daring her to open and let him inside.

But he didn't take. She would have to give. Whatever else she was, Maudie was special, and if this thing that was smoldering between them was going to be allowed to burst into flames, it had to be a mutual decision.

The daybed was hard and narrow. Keegan knew damned well she had a wide, comfortable mattress not thirty feet away, but it never occurred to him to try for it. Not because it would be too calculated a move, but because he honestly didn't think he could go the distance. He was starting to think he might have underestimated his control, something he had never had trouble with before.

"You cold?" he murmured against her ear.

She shuddered all over, and he knew a moment of sheer sensual power that he could do this for her. He could do far, far more if she would let him.

He brushed his hands over her hair, over the thick, silky, clover-scented skein that flowed down over her shoulders, and his hands moved down her back to her narrow waist, then lower, to curve over the generous swell of her buttocks. Hanging on by a thread, he pressed her against him, groaning at the exquisite sensation that hovered somewhere between pleasure and pain.

"It's going to be good, sweetheart," he vowed. "I promise, you won't regret it."

"Rich, are we going too fast? I'm afraid—"

"Don't be. Maudie, I'd never hurt you. I—"

And then he closed his eyes and swore silently for a long, long time. While she lay warm and trusting on top of him, the hard swell of his sex nestled in that special place at the top of her thighs, Keegan called himself every lousy name in the book, in several Arabic dialects. Because he had brought her this far—brought them both to the ragged edge and now he didn't have what it took to go through with it.

And he had a feeling she didn't, either.

Between his efforts and her wriggling, her gown was rucked up to her hips. It took almost more strength than he possessed, but Keegan reached down and began clumsily smoothing it back over her thighs.

Lifting her head from his chest, Maudie said, "Are you cold?"

"Hardly!" His bark of laughter rang out in the large, sparsely furnished room. "Honey, let me ask you a very personal question, okay?"

"Do you have to?"

"Yeah, I think I do. For your own sake."

"If it's about—you know—well, I don't. That is, I haven't. Not for a long, long time."

He could have wept. His arms tightened around her and he buried his face in her hair, rocking her gently on top of him until he realized that he was only making things worse for them both. "I know, sweetheart. Believe me, I wish my brain had short-circuited twenty minutes ago, but I started this, so I guess it's up to me to deal with it.''

"I wasn't thinking. You don't even know me, so how could you—''

Strangely enough, he didn't have the kind of doubts she obviously thought he had. He was thinking solely of her protection. And while he could assure her on one count, he had an idea she wouldn't exactly welcome the possibility of pregnancy.

"Hush, love,'' he murmured, covering her lips with his fingertip.

With a small sound of distress, she drew it into her mouth and sucked gently, driving him quietly out of his mind. When he could speak again, he said, "The thing is, I'm afraid I'm not dressed for the occasion. I, uh, hadn't planned on being over here more than a couple of hours.''

Besides which, when a man had been held captive, first in a foreign country, then in a series of hospitals, being hacked open, sewed up and dosed with muscle relaxants, sex wasn't exactly a prime priority. He'd got out of the habit of carrying protection.

They were both breathing heavily. Maudie's back felt chilled while her front side, the parts of her that were in intimate contact with Rich's body, were fiery hot. "I reckon we were both sort of taken by surprise,'' she whispered shakily. As if suddenly realizing that her hands were still toying with the velvety swirl of hair on his crown, she jerked them away, and Keegan caught them and drew them up to his lips. Moving with great care, he rolled over, taking her with him, and then swung one leg over her hips to hold her in place.

"Honey, I hate to disillusion you, but the first time I ever laid eyes on you, I started thinking about getting you in bed. That was before I saw your shotgun.''

There was a long moment of silence, and then Maudie laughed. At least it sounded slightly more like a laugh than a sob, although Keegan couldn't have sworn to it.

Neither could Maudie. "You told me I wasn't your type."

"I lied."

"Then if we're being honest, I may as well confess something, too. I—you—" She took a deep, shuddering breath. "That is, I've only dated twice in seven years, and that was six years ago. I haven't met anyone since then who was worth the trouble."

"Trouble?"

"Well, it didn't seem like a good idea to try a first date over here, in case things didn't work out. But if we met over there, then that would mean a boat trip back after dark—never my favorite thing. And so . . ." She shrugged, making him excruciatingly aware of just one of the advantages of short, well-rounded women. "You know what I mean."

He studied her quizzically in the faint, golden light. "That's it? End of confession? Honey, you had me all primed for something juicy."

Her laugh sounded breathless, but at least this time it was definitely a laugh. Swamped in a sudden wash of spontaneous tenderness, Keegan wanted to hug her, to tuck her under his wing, shoehorn her body into his and settle in for a long winter's nap. Trouble was, he was beginning to suspect that a long winter's nap wouldn't be enough. Which presented an altogether different kind of problem.

"No, what I meant to say was—well, I don't exactly know how to put this politely, but—well, here goes. I was curious, that is, I thought about—" One hand waved indecisively. "The thing is, I—"

"Wondered what it would be like to make love with me," he finished for her when it seemed as if she might expire before she could get it out.

"Sort of. Well, yes. I don't know exactly why. I mean, I never think about that sort of thing anymore. Very rarely. Almost never. I stay so busy what with my work and painting and just surviving, that it doesn't leave a whole lot of time for... hmm... fantasizing."

"I think you win."

"I do? Win what?"

"The honesty sweepstakes." Keegan squeezed her and reluctantly slid his leg off hers, leaving her free to escape if she wanted to, because he was just beginning to understand how much her freedom really meant to her.

For a moment she didn't move, and his good intentions wavered dangerously. There were ways. More ways probably than she had ever dreamed of in her wildest fantasy. With a bitter smile, he thought of the weeks he had hung on to his sanity by fantasizing about hot showers, clean beds, good food, and great sex and then reciting everything he had ever memorized from the first grade on up.

But this was no fantasy At this moment, with this woman, Keegan wanted it all. Wanted it all, wanted it now, and wanted it more than he had wanted anything in a long time. Which was a very good reason to pull out before he got in any deeper.

Then he wigged out completely. "Maudie, think about it, will you? Tomorrow I'm going over to Hatteras. I still need a bigger pry bar, but now there's another reason to go. So tomorrow after supper we'll pick up this discussion where we left off. Deal?"

Eyes wide, she scrambled backward and would have tumbled onto the floor if he hadn't caught her. "No way! And you needn't bother to buy any—you know. Because this was just a fluke. In fact, I think it's past time you were heading north again, don't you?''

Keegan told himself he was crazy. She'd put a spell on him. Either that or this damned Camelot-Coronoke Island of hers was doing things to his head. "No way," he heard himself saying. "I never liked leaving a job unfinished, and this is one—"

"I'm not a job!"

"No, you're not," he agreed, struggling to shut down certain systems and engage others. Primarily his brain. "I was talking about the Hunt. I've got some ideas I'd like to run by you if you have time tomorrow, something I think you might find interesting."

"I think you must be hallucinating," she retorted. "Brandy and turpentine evidently don't mix too well."

"You're the doctor."

"Right. And my new prescription is for a few hours of sleep, followed immediately by a move to a more northerly climate."

Keegan laughed and let her go, wondering if she had any idea how close he had come to losing it. Any idea how much control it had taken not to carry those small callused hands of hers down to where his body most desperately craved attention—to show her just how much pleasure a woman could give a man and a man could give a woman without any risk at all. Why hadn't he? They could have both enjoyed it with no regrets and no complications.

Crossing his arms beneath his head, he stared into the darkness for a long time after she'd gone, thinking of fate and family, and the unexpected turns a man's life could take just when he least expected it.

Maudie curled into a knot, her fingers pressed under her cheeks in a way that was bound to produce wrinkles. She had promised herself to stop sleeping that way, and for the past several months she'd been practicing sleeping on her back, a position which, according to Janine, would take ten years off her face by the time she reached sixty.

But at the first hint of insecurity, she always regressed to her old bad habits. Insecurity, in Maudie's case, usually involved a man. Which was funny, really, because two less similar men than Sanford Winters and Richmond Keegan would be hard to find.

Not that Rich wasn't a managing type, too, because he was. A blue ribbon chauvinist of the first degree. Evidently it had never once occurred to him that a woman who had been living alone on an island for nearly two years and managing quite well could get along without his interference, even when that interference was well meant.

As if she would even consider allowing herself to get involved with any man again. She might not have a college degree—something her ex-husband had been forever throwing up in her face, although he was the reason she didn't. But even a mouse could learn from experience, and Maudie prided herself on having at least as much common sense as the average field mouse. Experience had taught her that if she relied on herself, she would seldom be disappointed.

When she had first left Sanford, pregnant, scared, bruised and broke, her newly widowed father had opened his heart and his home. She'd had a hard time preventing him from going after the bastard who had so mistreated his daughter, but Maudie had had enough of violence to last her a lifetime.

Her father loved her, she had never once doubted that. He doted on Ann Mary to the point where Maudie had had to put her foot down to keep her daughter from being spoiled rotten. But when he had met Janine years later, he had fallen hard, and although Maudie knew she could have stayed on, she also knew it would have been unfair to Janine. Within a week she had made other arrangements that had worked out to the satisfaction of all parties involved.

No, Maudie didn't need anyone. She had supported herself and her daughter since Ann Mary was a baby, and she intended to go on doing just that. Rich might scoff at her makeshift setup, but it worked for her. She had a roof over her head, money in the bank, and family just over on the next island. There was food for the taking right outside her front door, and she didn't need a fancy wardrobe because there was no one she wanted to impress. She most certainly didn't need clothes to attract a man!

Oddly enough, it was from her stepmother that Maudie had gained final sanction for her new life-style. Janine had been married to a psychologist and had evidently picked up a few clues from the association before it had ended in divorce.

"There are four possible reasons why a woman might need a man," she had told Maudie shortly before she had married Medlin. "Sex, companionship, reproduction and financial security. I'm marrying your father for two out of four. Enough said."

Maudie was financially about as secure as anyone could be in her particular circumstances. At least what she didn't have, she couldn't lose. She had done her reproducing and was satisfied with the results. As for companionship, she was quite comfortable with her own company. She and Ann Mary were closer than most mothers and daughters. They always would be, no matter what. After Ann Mary was through school, Maudie was considering moving to the mainland and looking for work in the same area so that they could share an apartment. She had been saving up for just that event.

Meanwhile, if she got tired of her own company, she didn't have far to go to find friends and family.

Oh, yes, she told herself as she drifted off to sleep, she had everything a woman could need, plus the added security of knowing that a man she had once foolishly trusted enough to marry wasn't going to kick her physically out of his bed in the middle of the night and then pretend he'd been dreaming when they both knew better.

Hearing the creak of the daybed springs, she smiled in the darkness, straightened out her legs, and turned onto her back. After a while, a soft purr issued from her parted lips.

Keegan opened his eyes. His brain lagged two seconds behind, his body closer to five. He had once gone without sleep for forty-seven hours with no lasting ill effect, but he'd be the first to admit that he did a lot better on a minimum of five hours out of twenty-four.

He was feeling edgy. Unsettled. Part of the problem was precisely as old as the resignation of his commission in the air force. It stemmed directly from the fact that when a man had been active all his life, he was nowhere near ready to be put out to pasture at the age of forty-one and a half. Hell, he was just entering the prime of his life!

So what if a few of his reflexes weren't quite as sharp as they had been twenty years ago, or even ten? Experience counted for something, didn't it? So what if his back was never going to be too reliable? Dammit, cuts in the Pentagon budget were one thing, but cutting the heart right out of the nation's defence was another matter.

He sat up in bed, drawing up his knees and staring morosely at the knuckles on his fist. Nah, that wasn't the problem. One of his guiding principles had always been self-honesty. Whether he liked the results or not. There were times—and this was one of them—when he wished he didn't know himself quite so well. What had him racing his engines this morning wasn't the fact that he was hanging in limbo, his life's career suddenly at an end. What ailed him was no more and no less than the kind of nervous energy that accumulated in a man's system as a result of a bottlenecked libido.

On the other hand, energy was energy. If a man had it, he could either burn it constructively or risk having it burn holes in his gut.

Keegan studied the complex curves of the sagging ceiling while he turned over several possibilities in his mind. With the male's normal matutinal readiness, he considered slipping into bed with Maudie and—

Okay, so that was out. Nor was he quite ready yet to risk calesthenics. As for running, motion for motion's sake had never been his style. What he needed was to *accomplish* something!

The sky was beginning to change from gunmetal gray to tarnished brass when he glanced at his wrist, swore, shrugged, and swung out of bed, relieved and moderately surprised to feel nary a twinge in his back.

His conscience was another matter, but he was in no mood to deal with abstracts. He needed a project, and he needed it *now!* He could finish unloading the lumber he had hauled across. Or he could take Maudie's outboard and rescue his rental, which would mean a leisurely chug across the broad stretch of placid water.

Uh-uh. No way. Not unless that ugly, flat-bottomed skiff of hers had an after-burner hidden up its stern. After twenty years as a jet jockey, Mach zilch wasn't his style.

Forty minutes later, Keegan had assembled a large pile of rotted timbers and broken shingles, dragged out of the building using ropes, a thorough knowledge of physics and a moderate amount of brute force. All with no discernible damage to his back, thank God.

An hour later, just about the time the wind started to kick up, the pile was blazing nicely.

All it took was one sniff and Maudie hit the deck running. "Rich! Get out! Quick, get out of the house!" she screamed. Scooping up her boots, she ignored her bathrobe and raced into the next room.

The stove was cold. Even half asleep, she could tell that much, but that didn't mean anything. Evidently a spark— "Fire! Keegan, wake up!"

He was gone. Oh, God, where? Was he somewhere in this rabbit warren, trapped under a mess of rubble, watching helplessly while the flames crept closer and closer?

Heart jammed in her throat, she tore out of the house, following her nose and the ominous crackling sound. By hopping on first one foot and then the other, she managed to ram her feet into her boots. Holding her flapping nightgown up to keep from tripping, she raced around the corner of the house.

And there he was. Naked to the waist, slogging away at a blazing loblolly pine with his shirt, but blessedly alive.

Her heart tumbled back into place and she swallowed great gulps of smoky, pungent air. "Rich, get back! Are you crazy?" she screeched. Wheeling around, she ran toward the generator house, where she stored her firefighting equipment. "You are mad! Absolutely *mad!*" she ranted, dragging out a child's runnerless sled with a fire extinguisher, a bucket, several burlap bags, a shovel, an ax and a rake strapped to it.

Keegan was beside her before she got even halfway. He tried to take the sled reins from her hands, and she slugged him. "Move! Just get out of my way, will you? Dammit, nothing like this ever happened before you came barging into my life! Will you *leave me alone?* I've got a fire to put out!"

Calmly, Keegan lifted the extinguisher off the sled, checked the pressure gauge, and headed for the pine tree. "Start raking a clearing. I'll hit the shovel as soon as I wet down this tree. If the top catches, we're in big trouble."

"Keegan, give me that thing! You don't even know what you're doing!"

But it was already evident that he did. Maudie grabbed the rake and set to work. Ignoring the blaze at the middle of the pile of debris, she hurriedly cleared the perimeter of pine straw, and then Keegan, having exhausted the water in the pressurized container, was shoveling sand on the central blaze. The wind blew fitfully, first from one direction, then another. The sun was just climbing out of a bank of low-lying clouds.

After the third time she tripped on her gown, Maudie tore the ruffle off and tossed it away. If it weren't for the possibility of stepping on a hot coal, she'd have shed her flapping boots, as well.

Keegan kept a careful watch over her and she kept a careful watch on him, but neither of them spoke. They were too busy beating out small grass fires, too busy flogging saplings with wet burlap bags.

Then, before Maudie quite realized how it had happened, it was all over except for the odd curl of smoke from the center of the blackened timbers.

"You okay?" Keegan asked gruffly, coming to stand beside her. His chest, under a pelt of dark hair, was glistening with sweat, streaked with ashes, and suspiciously red in more than one area.

After one glance, Maudie dropped her gaze to the ground. No, she wasn't "okay," she was completely shattered. Not that she would ever admit it. "How on earth did it happen?"

"My damned stupidity."

She hadn't meant the fire. It was plain enough how that had happened. She would have told him if he'd bothered to ask that the only time to burn trash was just before a rain, only he hadn't asked, he had gone ahead and done it, just like he barged in and did everything without using the least bit of judgment. Men of action could be a royal pain.

"I'm wiped out."

"I don't wonder," he said.

But what bothered Maudie even more than the fire was her reaction to it. It had been years since she had lost control that way. Even now she couldn't believe she had pitched a genuine four-alarm tantrum. She *never* lost her temper!

Sanford would have loved it, she thought with bitter amusement. He would have taken exquisite pleasure in carving her up in tiny pieces and then inflicting small cruelties on the quivering remnants. And in case her personhood survived that, he had other, less subtle ways of getting to her.

"I'm sorry," she whispered as Keegan dropped an arm over her shoulder.

They were both sitting on one of the timbers he had dragged out to burn and then changed his mind, levering it off to one side. From the weight of the thing, it was only rotten on the surface. Trim off the dead wood and you'd have something a hell of a lot sounder than anything that could be bought today, he'd be willing to bet.

"I'm the one who needs to apologize. I should've cleared it with the boss before I tackled this project."

"Why didn't you?" she asked with a bleak little smile that cut right down to the quick.

"Boss was still snoring. I didn't have the heart to wake her."

With a grimy finger, she drew a series of overlapping circles in the sand. "Sorry again if my snoring woke you up."

He covered her hand with his, winced and drew it back. "You purr like a kitten."

"I'll bet. Rich, I don't usually go charging around that way, screaming my head off. I don't know what got into me."

"You're allowed. I pulled a damn fool stunt, and you reacted properly by chewing me out. That's a pretty adequate fire truck you've got there, by the way."

"Adequate?"

"Wheels might've helped."

"Not in the sand." She slanted a smile up at him, and Keegan closed his eyes against the powerful urge to gather her into his arms and kiss away the dirt, the sweat, and all the uncertainties he saw on her face. For a woman who was usually unflappable, she'd showed herself to be human. So what was the big deal?

"Okay. Better than adequate," he conceded.

"Thanks. Some of the volunteer firemen over on Hatteras Island helped me put it together. This is the first time I've ever had to use it."

"Better get your tank refilled and recharged."

"But first, I guess we'd better shovel more sand over your bonfire."

"Yeah. My bonfire..." Either they were talking on one level and communicating on another, or his imagination had gone into a power dive, Keegan thought, suddenly wary all over again. Just for a minute there, he'd thought she wanted to throw herself into his arms and hang on tight—the same way he wanted to hang on to her.

Reaffirmation. Natural reaction under the circumstances, he told himself. He'd seen perfect strangers climb all over each other coming out of a high stress situation. It didn't mean anything. Afterward, they were usually pretty embarrassed.

Maudie stood and reached for the shovel, only to have him remove it from her hands. Numbly, she allowed him to take it. She was reliving those first few moments when she had awakened, smelling smoke. Her first thought had been for Rich. And her next, and her next. Even now, when she had every right to be furious with him—when he was right here beside her, wet, filthy, but safe and secure in his strength—she quaked inside at the thought of what might have happened if he had gone exploring again and been trapped inside the rambling old ruin, and it had caught fire.

She told herself she would have been terrified for anyone under those circumstances. It was the only possible reaction. Yet she knew just as well as she'd ever known anything that there was a difference.

It was that difference that was was so scary. She didn't understand it, but she was too honest to deny it.

* * *

An hour later that same day, Maudie discovered Keegan trying to bandage his own right hand. "Oh, for goodness' sake, what have you done now?"

"Nothing," he muttered, giving her his shoulder. They were in the Hunt's only half-functioning bathroom. Instead of net, the big porcelain bathtub held a smaller galvanized washtub, a dipper and a plastic bucket.

"Let me see, Richmond."

"Stop bugging me, Maude."

"Then stop acting like a child, Colonel."

"A child! Lady, for your information, it's been forty damned years since anyone has accused me of acting like a child!"

"What's the matter, is your family too intimidated by your nasty temper?"

"Look who's talking about temper," Keegan jeered, and his guard slipped just enough so that she was able to take his hand in hers and unfold the fingers that were curved protectively over his palm.

The length of gauze fell unnoticed to the floor. "Oh, Rich—why didn't you tell me?" she said with a sigh.

"Because it's not worth talking about," he muttered.

"I've got a pretty good antiseptic, but you're going to have to be real careful not to let it get infected. Maybe we'd better take you over to see the doc—"

"I'll manage, okay?" He jerked his hand behind him. Dammit, why was it that ever since he'd laid eyes on this woman, he'd been pulling one crazy stunt after another? An officer in the USAF! A man other men looked to for leadership!

"Honestly, Rich, you need a keeper," Maudie murmured, reaching for his hand again, and her words came so close to echoing his own thoughts that Keegan lost it. Just plain out and out lost it.

"Look, forget it, will you? It's nothing!"

"Right across the creases of your palm, too. It's going to be the very devil to keep from breaking open while it heals."

"I'll manage," he said through clenched teeth. The clenched teeth were not on account of the pain, although the pain was excruciating. But, dammit, why did he always manage to end up looking like a dumb jerk? Was it something in the water?

Or was Maudie Winters out to get him?

Eight

"**I**f you're applying for the job, Ms. Winters, you're flat out of luck. I'm not in the market for another wife."

Maudie was still holding Keegan's hand palm up in hers. She stared up at him indignantly. Like an evil genie, the temper she had crammed back into its bottle began to billow up once more. "If I'm— You're not— A *wife!*"

"On the other hand, if you're willing to settle for something a little less formal, I'll be glad to offer you my fullest cooperation."

She slammed the back of his hand down on the edge of the lavatory and grabbed his wrist. He could have easily broken her hold, but for some reason, he didn't. "Good. Great! I'll settle for your fullest cooperation in getting off my island and out of my sight! Is that informal enough for you?"

With her free hand, Maudie thrust open the mirrored door of the brass and mahogany wall cabinet and snatched a tube of antiseptic. "You don't know just how tempted I am to let your whole arm rot and drop off," she muttered. "You are without a doubt the biggest—the biggest—"

"Hero?"

"*Rock head* I have ever had the misfortune to meet!"

Keegan smiled, the planes of his face flattening out in that feline way she had noticed before. "Why, thank you."

She twisted off the cap and it rolled onto the floor. Swearing, she squeezed out a two-inch blob of translucent jelly and tossed the tube aside. "If you're going to be sarcastic, you can damn well doctor your own stupid hand! I've got better things to do!" Each phrase was underlined by a hard circular stroke of her thumb as she applied the ointment to the reddened area of his right palm.

Maudie was simmering.

No, she wasn't. She was at a full, rolling boil! She couldn't remember the last time she had been so steaming mad!

Or so alive, her subconscious whispered.

Silently, Keegan endured the dichotomy of feelings as long as he could and then he shut his eyes and prayed his body wouldn't embarrass him too much.

Or if it did, that she would be too angry to notice.

Think cold showers, man!

Instead he thought soft, tumbled beds, warm, willing bodies, and long, fantastic nights filled with exquisite pleasure.

With a groan, he opened his eyes and stared down at the top of her head. She was doing it deliberately, damn her. It had to be deliberate, because no woman, not even a female hermit, could be that naive.

"Do you have the least idea what this kind of thing does to a man?" he gritted through clenched jaws.

"I hope it hurts like hell," she shot back, but the anger was not quite so evident in the throbbing huskiness of her voice as she continued to stroke his palm with slow, circular movements. Up and down, and then sideways—and then around and around again.

Keegan breathed raggedly through his mouth. He was dying. Parts of him felt like ice, parts of him felt like fire, and the parts that were hot were getting hotter by the moment. "Enough," he grated, jerking his hand from her grasp.

She lifted her face. Her eyes collided with his and clung. There was a streak of soot across one of her cheeks from chin to temple, and with his good hand, Keegan reached up and smeared it. Her skin was like wet satin. Damp, silky—flushed from exertion.

"Your shoulder," she murmured, but neither of them spared a glance for his singed and smut-streaked shoulder.

Keegan shuddered. He swallowed hard. "It's nothing. How about you? Any spots that need attention?"

Maudie could have named several right off the bat, but she didn't think that was what he'd meant.

Or was it?

She told herself she was acting out of character, then rationalized that it was only because they had come so close to disaster. That's all it was. All it could possibly be, because she wasn't the type to get upset. She *never* raised her voice. If anyone had a temper, it was Keegan, yet he had been calm as ice until the fire was out, even though he must have been in excruciating pain.

He was still in pain, Maudie reminded herself, and she was acting like the worst kind of a witch. The man had just saved her home and quite possibly the entire island.

Of course, he'd been the one to endanger them in the first place, but that was beside the point.

His hand was still on her cheek. Closing her eyes, she sighed. "I yelled, didn't I? I'm sorry."

Keegan's right hand fell to her shoulder and then both arms went around her. One hand—his good one—began stroking her back.

If he meant the gesture to be comforting, he was missing the mark by a country mile. Maudie was brimming over with . . . with something. The dregs of all the excitement, probably. Or possibly a residue of what had almost happened the night before. Whatever it was, it was not *comfort* that was causing all those melting urges that made her want to do something totally reckless.

She could have pulled away. Should have. Instead she swayed forward to lean her forehead against his chest, which was a big mistake. Because she was suddenly shatteringly aware of the heat of his body. The heavy beat of his heart. The contrasting textures of crisp, damp hair and hard, satiny skin.

He was salty. So was she. He was breathing hard . . . so was she.

"Maudie?"

"I didn't—I'd better—"

"Maudie, this is nuts. After what just happened—after last night—but right now I want you so much it hurts like hell." He assayed a small laugh that ended in a groan. "So if you want to yell some more, this might be a good time to do it."

The trouble was, she didn't want to yell. She wanted to slide her hands down his sweat-slick, smoky-smelling sides to his belt, and work her way around to the buckle, and then tackle the zipper on his ruined trousers.

And then . . .

"Maudie?" His right arm held her close—as if she needed any help—while his left one came around so that he could tilt her face up to his. Like a dark, glistening warrior cast in living bronze, he stared down at her, his eyes dark with desire. "This is your captain speaking," he said huskily. "All ashore that's going ashore."

Maudie closed her eyes and parted her lips. She wasn't going ashore. Wherever her captain—her colonel—was going, she was going, too, because quite suddenly, she couldn't see any other possible course.

With a ragged laugh, Keegan said, "I think this is the place where we're supposed to climb into a nice warm shower together and take turns working each other into a lather."

She was already worked into a lather. "I'll pump you a bucket of cold water. That's the best I can offer."

"Somehow, cold water doesn't interest me at the moment. I know another way of putting out fires."

But Keegan's other way didn't put out any fires—not for a long, long time, at least. It took place in her bed and involved a kettleful of water heated on the gas ring, a basin, and a damp, soapy cloth. Maudie took the cloth from his hand as the fire threatened to blaze up out of control. First she bathed his face and neck, paying particular attention to his ears. She inspected them closely, her warm breath causing him to inhale sharply.

"Turn over onto your stomach" she commanded.

"I'm not sure that's possible."

He managed, drawing one knee up for support, and carefully, she washed his broad, tapering back, stroking and kneading the hard muscles there. There were reddened areas, but none that required further attention. Her palm slid lingeringly down the valley of his spine and her fingertips edged under his belt.

Keegan swore under his breath and rolled over onto his back again. "You don't know a lot about damage control, do you?"

Maudie knew more about damage control than she'd thought. She knew, for instance, that control was the farthest thing from her mind at the moment. Carefully, she explored his chest, the sharp rise of his rib cage, the pattern of hair that swirled around his small, erect nipples and trailed lower in a narrow stripe. Keegan, his eyes closed tightly, alternately gasped and swore.

Maudie only smiled, her composure fully restored. Sitting cross-legged on the bed beside him, she dropped the cloth in the pan of cooling water and had just reached for his belt buckle when his good hand came down over hers.

Keegan's eyes snapped open. "All systems fully armed and ready," he said tersely. "This might go down as the briefest sortie on record."

"I don't understand."

"No? Then you'll just have to trust me, won't you?"

Rising, he took the cloth from her hand, dropped it into the basin and left the room. Maudie watched him go, her gaze moving down his broad, tapering back to the taut, blue-clad muscles below his belt.

She wanted him naked. Naked in her bed. Images that would have been beyond her wildest dreams—or her worst nightmares—only a few days ago, suddenly weren't.

A moment later he returned with a basin full of clean, warm water. Using the same cloth Maudie had used on him, he commenced with her forehead and slowly, lingeringly, attentively worked his way south. By the time he had reached as far inside as was possible, the neck of her ruined flannel gown was drenched and Maudie was all but weeping. Her nipples tightened against the grimy, rosesprigged material, trembling visibly with every beat of her pounding heart.

"I've always had a secret desire to rip a nightgown off a beautiful woman's body," Keegan confessed.

The smile she gave him was blended of sadness, wistfulness and amusement. It just about tore the heart right out of him.

"Sorry. Short women with Napoleon complexes probably don't qualify, but if you need a gown to practice on, be my guest. I don't think this one's got many more miles left in it, anyway."

With a soft groan, Keegan leaned over, smoothing her tangled hair off her face, and lowered his mouth to hers. Hovering there, he whispered, "You qualify. If moonlight shafting through towering cumulus formations is beautiful. Or—" his lips settled on hers for an instant "—sun glinting on a lazy, twisting river. Or—" His tongue engaged hers in a brief flurry of activity, and then he lifted his head and smiled down at her, his face flushed in a way that Maudie didn't think was entirely due to his recent firefighting activities.

"Or a crusty skilletful of cornbread?" she suggested in a desperate attempt to delay the headlong plunge into the unknown. On the brink, she suddenly panicked. She needed time to think! Needed it, but didn't want it, which made it all the more imperative that she slow up.

But it was too late to slow up. When Keegan buried his face in her throat, she closed her eyes and held him tightly.

"Will you be cold?" he asked several moments later. "I'm not sure I want to take a chance on building up the fire. At least, not the one in the stove," he added with a shaky laugh.

"We could make a bedroll of these quilts."

"Too confining. I need room to operate." As if to prove it, he rolled over and reached out to the table that held her mending basket, fumbling for her scissors.

Maudie watched uncertainly as he turned toward her with the gleaming blades. "Rich? Uh, what kind of operating are we talking about?"

He chuckled, and the sound played on her spine like the bass notes of a pipe organ. "Not what you're thinking. Honey, as romantic as it sounds, tearing nightgowns off is tough duty for all concerned without a little help."

"I could always just pull it off over my head."

"Don't be a spoilsport. I'm just going to make it easier by cutting through this whatchamacallit up here at your neckline."

"You're the expert."

"Sorry to disillusion you, but I've never done this before. Always wanted to, though, so indulge me, will you?"

She indulged him. While Keegan carefully clipped through the layers that bound the neckline of her ruined flannel gown, Maudie watched his frown of concentration, watched the play of sunlight through the salt-clouded window on his angular face, his powerful shoulders—the glint of gray in his dark blond hair. Her eyes moved over him hungrily. She was pretty sure he was delaying the moment, giving her time to change her mind. For a big, aggressive, hot-tempered chauvinist, he could be amazingly considerate.

She wasn't going to change her mind. Not in a million years.

The sound of ripping cloth was loud in the quiet room. Chill air whispered over her naked body an instant before Rich came down over her, drawing the covers up over them both. "No fair," she said. "I didn't get to cut anything off you."

He winced. "Lady, don't even think about it!"

She laughed aloud, and so did he, and she thought wonderingly what a lovely mixture laughter and sex could be.

In a fleeting memory, she saw herself as a young wife, eager, uncertain, so afraid of being physically hurt, and later of being left high and dry by an insensitive husband who quickly saw to his own pleasure and instantly fell asleep.

They'd been crazy to get married when they did—medical students' lives were not their own. But as she had learned later to her sorrow, Sanford was given to doing crazy, impulsive things, and she had been too young and inexperienced to know better.

She heard Rich gasp and realized he had touched her with his right hand. "I'm sorry," she whispered.

"No, sweetheart, I am. If ever there was a time when I wanted two good hands, it's now. With you."

Maudie's heart melted. If she had had a single reservation, it melted right along with it, because Rich was no Sanford Winters. Whatever else he was, he was a good man, a kind man—a man to whom other people were important.

And she was no shallow, impressionable girl, to fall for a handsome face and a smooth line, fully expecting to live happily ever after. She had long since learned that not all fairy tales came true. But if there was a chance for a happy here-and-now, Maudie didn't intend to waste a single moment of it, because those moments were too rare in her experience. She would deal with tomorrow...tomorrow.

"Let me help you," she murmured, her hands moving under the covers to the silver buckle of his narrow leather belt. "One-handed, there are some things a man just can't manage alone."

"Oh, I expect I could, even with no hands at all."

The buckle undone and her fingers on the fastener at the top of his zipper, she wrestled her face out from under the covers and found his eyes. They were glinting in wicked amusement. "Are you by any chance talking naughty?"

"Would you recognize it if I were?"

"I'm hardly inexperienced."

"No, but you've been living in this cocoon for how long now?"

"Long enough to know that we're going to have to risk letting some cold air inside this cocoon or we'll never get you out of your pants."

Keegan's brows shot up comically. "And you accused me of talking naughty?"

With a sound that came close to a giggle, Maudie reached her arms up and drew him down on top of her. "Did anyone ever tell you you're a thoroughly nice man, Colonel Keegan?"

Keegan studied the sudden moisture that sparkled on her lashes.

He felt a stab of something that had nothing at all to do with desire. "Believe me, sweetheart, the last thing a man wants to be called at a time like this is nice, so do me a favor..."

He lowered his lips to hers, tilted his head and kissed her hard and deep while his good hand cleared away the scraps of torn flannel that still clung to her naked body under the covers. Then, palming her breast, he tested the fullness, the softness, the sensitivity of the hardened peak, glorying in the way she arched to him when he circled it with his fingertips.

Her legs entwined with his, and she kicked vigorously until his pants—belt, briefs and all—were at the foot of the bed. By that time, her activity had nearly brought him past critical mass to the point of core meltdown.

"Last chance," he whispered roughly against her breast.

"Oh, please," Maudie whimpered, and he felt her thighs parting, making room for him to settle into place. Between them they were generating enough heat to turn the island into a tropical zone.

"Don't be surprised if you see palm trees sprouting tomorrow," he said, reaching down to cover her mound with his good hand. She was narrow and hot, her petals delicately formed, and he parted her reverently. "Maudie, I— Ahh-hh!"

He shifted, and with one fierce thrust, he sank into her, paused for an instant, and then it was too late. She began to convulse around him, and he thrust again. Once, twice, three times.

And then he shuddered. "God, I'm sorry, love!"

"I couldn't wait," she gasped. "It's never happened before— Don't know why I... Ohh-hh, Rich." Eyes closed, Maudie collapsed.

Sometime later when she opened her eyes again, there was no hint of disorientation, even though it was broad daylight and she never slept during the day. She knew instantly where she was—and why—even though it had been more than half a lifetime since she had slept in a man's arms.

Strictly speaking, she never had slept in a man's arms. Sanford had never been a cuddler. Rich obviously was. His arm must have fallen asleep hours ago, but when she tried to ease away, it tightened around her. Their legs were so intertwined it was hard to tell where one body ended and the other began.

"Need to make a call?" he asked sleepily.

"No. Yes. I'm just not used to—"

"Neither am I, but I could easily grow accustomed."

"Yes, well . . ." She slipped out of bed and made a dash for the bathroom, conscious of Rich's eyes following her naked progress. There were certain disadvantages to making love in broad daylight and to having one's nightgown ripped off one's bare body, Maudie thought ruefully. Especially when one's legs were too short and one's bottom was too wide.

There was no way she could avoid returning to the bedroom, even if she'd wanted to, because that was where her clothes were. The trouble was, when she returned, he was waiting for her. Laying for her, like a big, sleepy, sexy tomcat. She could almost hear the purr in his voice as he asked her to glance at his hand.

"Let me get dressed first."

"Now."

"Rich, it'll just take a minute." She was holding a towel in front of her. Her backside was freezing.

"Come get under the covers where it's warm, and we'll play doctor, okay?"

"I trust you about as far as I'd trust a cottonmouth in the springtime," she shot back, half laughing, half serious.

"Why springtime?"

"Fresh out of hibernation, they're surlier than ever."

"Speaking of snakes, did you ever read Freud?"

"You mean the famous herpetologist?"

"Yeah, that's the one," Keegan said, chuckling. He lunged and caught her by the wrist, as she had meant to be caught, and in an instant she was back under the covers, sharing the heavenly warmth, as well as the musky and slightly smoky scent of two healthy adult bodies.

She was drunk on it. Drunk on him. Even knowing it, there wasn't a single thing she could do about it, even if she'd wanted to. "This is decadent," she protested weakly.

"What, sleeping with caretakers? If it's good enough for Lady Chatterly, it's good enough for me. I'm no snob."

"I meant, sleeping with your clothes," Maudie teased. Hooking his pants with her foot, she brought them up and tossed them at a chair. "What happened to the man who complained because he couldn't have his underwear starched and ironed?"

"You're the one who didn't want me to open up our nice snug cocoon long enough to shove 'em out. When in Rome..."

And then he smiled, his hair falling forward as he leaned over to nuzzle the tip of her nose with his. "But, hey—I did, didn't I? I ripped open the cocoon and took out the beautiful butterfly. And you are beautiful, Maudie. Don't ever let any man tell you you're not."

Any man?

A fleeting shadow crossed her mind, but before she could explore it, she was distracted by the things he was doing to her ears. And to her breasts. And then to the soft hollows of her body, laying open the covers and letting chilly sunshine spill across them both.

A long time later, Maudie roused again. She stretched, blinked several times and studied the unfamiliar angle of the slanting sunlight on the cherry-paneled wall.

It came back gradually at first, then all in a rush. Keegan—the fire. His hand, and what happened next.

And then what had happened again.

"Oh, Lord," she murmured, sinking back onto her pillow.

He was gone. He might still be on the island, but he was gone from her bed, and Maudie had no intention of chasing him down. She had too much pride to admit, even to herself, that she could fall in love with the kind of man who would ruin every cast-iron frying pan a woman owned, a man she couldn't get along with for five consecutive minutes...unless they were making love.

Rich pulled in at the marina and awkwardly tossed a line around a piling with his left hand. Driving with a stick shift was going to be a real pain, too, but he would manage. He had a lot of thinking to do, and he thought best when he was strapped into a cockpit, cruising at about Mach .9. It was a good, mind-freeing speed.

This time he wore wheels, not wings. Knowing he was not up to standard, he kept it down. At a plodding 45 mph, he cruised up beyond Avon and parked at a drive-out on the ocean side of the island. Locking his car, he crested the dunes and paused. A stiff northeast wind blew his clothes against his body, and he leaned into it, savoring the feel of pitting his strength against the elements even to this small extent. He'd be the first to admit that he had lived on adrenaline all his adult life. Most pilots did. All fighter pilots did. It went with the territory.

It was also an addiction. He knew that, too. There would always be a part of him, no matter how old he grew, that would delight in pitting himself against the odds.

But no man could live forever on the heady mixture of jet fuel and adrenaline. Keegan, with that same situation awareness that had made him the best at what he did while he was doing it, had known the instant he had lost his edge. It had happened about ten seconds after he had pulled the plug and discovered his chute was out of control and he was headed for a damned hard landing.

That time it had been the equipment that had failed.
Next time, it might have been the man. He had accepted it,
and even come to terms with it. Not while the rage was still
in him, while he was being carted around torn, bleeding
and feverish, from one prime target area to another as
propaganda bait.

But later. Lying on his belly in a hospital bed, with too
much time on his hands. He had accepted it—even come
to terms with it. The warriors who didn't die in battle always did, one way or another.

But something was missing from his life. Not flying.
One day soon, he would do that again. It was something
else, and it was beginning to bug the hell out of him. Reason told him he had more than a lot of poor devils ever
had. He had a family. He had his health. Money was no
problem. He had proved more than once last night that he
was was still capable of satisfying a woman, not to mention satisfying himself beyond his wildest dreams.

So what the hell was bugging him? Maudie?

It couldn't be Maudie. Sure, she was one terrific lady. So
terrific, in fact, that he was going to be sorry to leave her,
and that was a first. It had been a long time since he'd met
any woman he couldn't walk away from without a second
thought. The choice was still his. He was still in control.
Underneath that hot surface temper that bled off pressure
like a pop-off valve, there had always been a core of cold
steel.

So he would walk away. She would come out on top,
because by the time he left, that dump she lived in would
be fit to take in boarders if she wanted to.

At the very least, she wouldn't have to worry about its
falling in on her head.

So the problem wasn't Maudie. His conscience clear on
that count, Keegan turned away from the pounding surf

and walked back over the dune. Spotting a pay phone on his way south, he veered in to place a call.

"Hello, Ken! Any new crises demanding my personal attention?"

He was amused at the instant denial. It no longer bugged him that his family had deliberately schemed to get him off their backs. In their place, he would probably have done the same.

"Yeah, well—" Rich said, finally breaking into a recital of chest colds, orthodontists' bills, pregnant secretaries and local politics. "Look, everything's under control down here. I mean, no problem with the property or anything like that, but I thought I might hang around a week or so longer, sort of see if anything can be salvaged."

His attention strayed to watch a few nondescript birds tackle half a discarded sandwich, and he reminded himself to pick up a few groceries—maybe something that would appeal to a ring-tailed, four-legged panhandler.

"Dammit, nothing's going on! No, I don't need you to get the lawyers involved—no, no Realtors, either. Yeah, right. Look, I'll handle it, okay? Uh-huh. Right. Her name is Winters, a Mrs. Winters. Yeah—yeah, sure... Look, she's not a problem. Right. Look, Ken, I've gotta run, okay? This wind down here cuts right through to the bone. My love to all the family, and tell Edie I'll be back home to take care of that jungle in her backyard by the time the snow melts, all right?"

On the drive to the marina, he scanned the dial hoping to catch a news broadcast. Maybe that was it. A simple acid deficiency. His gut didn't pump enough acid when he couldn't sweat out the latest international crisis.

Chuckling, he listened to a fragment of some country-western ballad about empty rooms and long, lonesome nights before giving up on finding any news.

Lonesome. The word echoed in his mind as he passed the lighthouse road and drove through the wooded village of Buxton. It was the kind of word you seldom heard outside country songs. Up in his neck of the woods, the word was lonely, not lonesome. Lonesome sounded sort of Southern. Sort of desolate. About two notches bluer than lonely.

Was Maudie lonesome? Would she welcome him back with open arms?

Or with her shotgun?

It occurred to Keegan that it might be a good idea to lay out a few ground rules before things went any further. If there was one thing he had learned from his brief starring role as a husband it was that he didn't have the right qualifications. His career could have been partly responsible—servicemen had several strikes against them going in. Or maybe it was just him. It still added up to bad risk.

Hell, if he'd been looking to settle down again, he'd do better to look up Alice and talk her into giving them another chance. At least he would be in no danger of losing his self-respect by letting a woman walk all over him. As it turned out, all Alice had wanted from him was a large dose of financial security, which was a relatively small price to pay.

But you take a woman like Maudie, Keegan mused—a woman like Maudie would never settle for less than complete surrender. No way was he ever going to put himself through that again. Being a prisoner of war was bad enough. Being a prisoner in a bad marriage was not in the cards, not for him.

So the first thing he would do when he got back, he decided as he pulled into the parking lot at the Red and White and dug out his shopping list, was to lay down a few ground rules. If the woman was anywhere near as smart as he thought she was, she'd be the first to agree. Maudie had been around the block a time or two herself. If she'd been looking to try her luck again, she would hardly have holed up alone on a deserted island.

So, Keegan thought with satisfaction, they were agreed on that much, at least. The rest he could handle as it came up.

No sweat.

Nine

Keegan's resolutions met their first test when he pulled up to the pier late that afternoon to find Maudie waiting for him.

"Hi. I wasn't sure if you'd remember to get bacon or not, so if you didn't, I'll soak out some salt mullet for breakfast tomorrow."

Bacon? Salt mullet? There was a brittleness about her smile that spoke of uncertainty, and a few more resolutions melted away. He cut to the chase. "You knew I'd be back. I left all my gear behind as security."

"Oh, but I didn't—"

"Maudie—don't sweat it." And then, as if they were no more than friendly neighbors, he began setting the sacks of groceries on the pier. "I got a bunch of stuff. Couple of pounds of that coffee you liked, four more gallons of bottled water, a couple of T-bones, some baking potatoes and sour cream to go on 'em and a bottle of wine. Oh, yeah, and some salad stuff.''

Over the years Keegan had been through a lot of morning-afters, both before and after his marriage. He couldn't remember a single time when he had felt the way he felt now. Edgy. Wary. No flight plan, faulty controls, and no chute. ''Maybe I should have left a note,'' he said, knowing damned well why he hadn't. Wondering if she knew, too.

He hadn't been ready to talk about it. He'd had a funny feeling about this whole business ever since he'd woken up and seen her there, sound asleep, making that soft little puffy noise with her lips.

For a long time he had just lain there and watched her, thinking such things as, what if he hadn't come south to check out the Hunt? What if he'd simply come across to the island, checked it out and then left without trying to take anything away?

What if he had never laid eyes on this small, soft woman with her green eyes, her wide, sweet mouth, her tough, graceful little hands—a woman who packed all the wallop of a brace of Sidewinders?

''Here, these two aren't heavy,'' he said gruffly, handing over the sacks that held bread and fresh vegetables. Just as if she'd never done anything more strenuous than wave off a swarm of butterflies.

Not until the groceries were all put away did Maudie work up enough nerve to hand Keegan a pair of tweezers, a needle, and a bottle of Spirits of Camphor. ''Rich, I hate to bother you, but I have this, uh, problem?''

The whole time they'd been working, she had been in agony, knowing the wicked little beast was burrowing deeper and deeper into her tender behind with every second.

Keegan slipped out of his heavy leather coat and slung it over a chair back. "Anything I can help with, just say the word."

"Actually, I was headed over to see Janine when you pulled up. I was going to ask her, but if you don't mind..."

"So much for my welcoming committee. I thought you were just eager to see me again." His words were teasing, but something about the look in his eyes made her sorry she had even mentioned Janine.

He glanced at the equipment in her hands. "Got a splinter, right?"

"Worse. A tick."

"In January?"

"It's been a mild winter."

He took the things from her and waited. She stared unhappily at a point somewhere above and to the left of his left shoulder. If last night had never happened, this might not have been so embarrassing.

Yes it would. But it was either that or risk Rocky Mountain spotted fever. Or Lyme disease. Or a fit of screaming meemies. "It's on my bottom," she blurted miserably. "I've tried mirrors and everything, and I can't get hold of him, so if you don't mind too much, would you please just—do it?" Unsnapping her jeans, she turned and bent over the kitchen table. If he laughed—if he said one single word, she would die.

No. First she would murder him, and then she would die! "So much for independence," she muttered under her breath. When she felt his hands gently sliding her jeans and underpants down around her knees, she squinched her eyes shut, gritted her teeth and tried to pretend she was a thousand miles away.

Anywhere, doing *anything,* rather than here sprawled across a kitchen table while a stranger who knew every secret of her thirty-eight-year-old body dug a tick out of her derriere. God must truly have it in for her.

"You want me to dab some of this stuff in the bottle on after I chase the little devil out of paradise, right?"

"No, darn it, I want you to hold the bottle against my— against where he is long enough to encourage him to let go, and then—"

"Drown him, you mean?"

"Whatever. And then I want you to drag him out of there without leaving a single speck behind, but most of all, I don't want you to say another word. Ever. Just do it and forget it!"

"Yes, ma'am. Duty is my middle name. My lips are sealed."

Maudie, her head cradled sideways on her right arm, could have sworn she detected laughter in his voice, but not for a tax-free fortune would she turn and look. Oh, God, she hated bugs above all things in this world, and ticks more than any other bug, even wasps. Even cockroaches!

She smelled the camphor, felt the slight pressure of the bottle against her skin, and wondered what he was looking at.

If he were any sort of gentleman at all, he would be looking out the window, at least until the last possible moment.

"I think I just saw him go down for the third time. Ready for stage two?"

"Just do it," she said through clenched jaws.

It took even more time than the drowning, but at last Keegan stepped back and held the tweezers triumphantly aloft. "Score one for the good guys."

Maudie grabbed her britches and dragged them up, clutching them together as she peered suspiciously over her shoulder. "You're sure the head's not still in there?"

"My orders were to leave no incriminating evidence, uh, behind."

"Just so you're sure. I can't bear the thought of having bug parts embedded in my body." She shuddered and mumbled an embarrassed thanks, and Keegan deposited the tick in the stove, the wickedly teasing light in his eyes changing imperceptibly to something more tender.

"Actually, it's Harrison," he said.

"What's Harrison?" She zipped her placket and settled her layered shirts down over her hips.

"My middle name. I was lying when I told you it was Duty. Harrison was the name of my mother's godfather. He owned a fleet of jewelry stores in Maine and Rhode Island, and she sort of hoped he'd remember me in his will, but he left it all to his mistresses. Divided it all up among the five of 'em. Family pitched a fit, but they couldn't break the will. He was too wily to—"

"Rich, I don't believe a word of it, but thanks for trying to take my mind off my, uh, embarrassment. You could have laughed."

"Officer and gentleman. Code of honor, clause twenty-seven, item five—an officer and a gentleman never laughs at a lady when her tail's caught in a crack. Items five-A through five-M cover variations. Item five-C, for instance, covers an interesting variation concerning elevator shafts and pantyhose."

Maudie exploded. She laughed until her eyes were streaming, sobering only when Keegan tilted his head and said, "You expecting company?"

"N-no, not that I know of. Not until the last week of March. Hawk's Nest is rented for the entire month, starting the last of February."

"Stay here, I'll check it out."

But she was right behind him. By the time she recognized Jerry, she was loping down the last stretch of path. Jerry never came over unless he had a message to deliver in person. She had been saving up for a cellular phone. Until then, she made do with an old CB radio, which was unreliable whenever the skip was bad, which was most of the time here on the coast.

"My father," she whispered, lifting stricken eyes to Keegan's. "He has this heart thing."

He wrapped an arm around her shoulder and held her close while the small boat idled up to the pier. "Never borrow trouble. Let me handle this," he said quietly. "What's up?" he called a few moments later, reaching out with his good hand to catch the line.

"Call come in. I tried to raise you on the radio, Maudie, but you must not've been monitoring."

Maudie's heart shot up to her throat and lodged there. Keegan squeezed her tightly against his side, as if his physical support could change fate itself.

"It's not Daddy?" she whispered.

"No, Medlin's fine. That is, he's had this flu that's going around, but it's not him. Ann Mary—she was in this wreck."

Maudie stepped bravely away from Keegan's support, but then she reached back and grabbed his hand in a vise-like grip.

His right hand. "Oh, please, God, no," she prayed as a damp northeast breeze chilled her to the bone.

"She's okay. That is, this guy that called from Norfolk General said she was stove up some, but—"

Later it occurred to Keegan that for a woman who pretended to be indomitable, Maudie Winters was a fraud and a fake. It hadn't taken five minutes to settle the details. She had been all for diving into the boat with Jerry, hitching a ride up to Buxton, borrowing her father's truck and high-tailing it to Norfolk, until Keegan had stepped in.

"Go pack. You'll want to be prepared to stay a few days if you need to."

"Keegan, I don't have time to—"

"Do as I say, Maudie. You're not thinking clearly. With all due respect to your father's truck, we're taking my car. You're in no condition to drive anywhere. You're falling apart."

"But—"

"I'll secure things around here while you get ready to go."

"But I—"

"Maudie, you're wasting time."

"Dammit, you have no right to just walk in here and start issuing orders like some—"

"Do you want to go with me, or do you want to stay here and argue over rights?"

He saw her crumple, saw the fight go right out of her, and for just an instant he was tempted to give in and let her do it her way.

No, damn her stubborn, tick-ridden hide, she *needed* him! Right now she needed him to think for her, because she wasn't thinking clearly. She needed him to drive her, else she'd probably end up in a ditch. Or hauled in for speeding. She needed him to be there for her no matter what lay ahead, and regardless of whether or not she wanted his support, she was damned well going to get it!

Forty-five minutes later they were headed north on Highway 12. Music spilled into the quiet interior from one of several new CDs Keegan had purchased for the trip south.

Both hands steady on the wheel, he cut his eyes at her and saw that she was staring grimly ahead, fists clenched in her lap. A daughter. Her only child. There was no way he could shield her if things went sour, but he could be there.

When they stopped by the neat, white, frame house to leave word with her father, Keegan discovered where Maudie got her flawless olive skin. Her father's complexion was the same rich shade, only considerably more lined.

He was not a tall man, Maudie's father, though he gave that impression. Carrying himself with an innate dignity despite red-rimmed eyes and a hacking cough, he greeted them at the door, his dark eyes moving speculatively from Keegan to Maudie.

Keegan stood by, ready to defend, to protect, to explain or whatever else might be necessary. Stood by, hell—he hovered! But by then Maudie had recovered enough of her own composure to deal with her father's fears. "She's all right, Daddy. That much we do know. She probably called Jerry because she knew you'd been sick and didn't want to worry you. She'd hardly be doing that if it—if she—"

"My poor baby," the older man said several times. "My poor sweet little girl."

"I'll call you just as soon as I see her, Daddy, all right? Now, for goodness' sake," Maudie said while her stepmother scribbled frantically, "get back inside out of the cold. Janine, make him look after himself, will you?"

The older woman, an attractive redhead who hadn't begun life that way, Keegan would be willing to bet, shoved a list at her stepdaughter. "Here's a few things I really need, Maudie, if you have time to shop. What with Medlin's being sick with the flu, I haven't had chance to get to town since before Christmas. I missed all the sales."

Maudie stared at the slip of paper until Keegan took it and shoved it into her shoulder bag.

It was due to him she'd even remembered to bring a purse. He had also been the one to pack for her, choosing a dress, a sweater, a spare pair of jeans and a few shirts when she would have settled for nightgown and toothbrush.

"Tell me about Ann Mary," he said after they'd left the village of Buxton behind. Rain clouds sagged overhead. To the left, the Pamlico raced before the wind, while on the right, a gray surf flung spume high above the dunes.

"She's the most precious thing in my life," Maudie said quietly.

Keegan had pretty well figured that much out for himself. "So how come she's Ann Mary instead of Mary Ann?"

"What? Oh, I—" She sighed and, reaching over, Keegan unclasped the hands she'd been twisting together. The burn in his own right palm throbbed fiercely. Mentally, he cut off the pain at his wrist. It was the best he could do for now.

"My grandmother was Mary Ann. Hers was Ann Mary. Every few generations, the name flipflops. In between, we have Maudes and Adelines and—is this as fast as this thing will go?"

"We're doing five over the limit. Getting stopped for speeding isn't going to save us any time. What's she like?"

"Beautiful. Sweet. Kind. Wonderful. My best friend. We've always been close."

"And that's an objective appraisal, right?"

She chuckled, and Keegan felt as if he'd just done something heroic.

"All right, you want the truth? She's the most wonderful little girl any mother could wish for, but she's had her moments. For instance, when she was four and a half, I washed her mouth out with soap every day for a week for using bad words. Come to find out, she liked the taste of soap.''

It was Keegan's turn to laugh.

"She's beautiful—or did I already say that? She used to sleep with a wooden boat Daddy made her instead of her dolls. She likes music and chocolate and she adores her granddaddy. I was hoping she'd want to teach—I think she still might, but first she wants to travel. I know it's selfish of me, but I hate the thought of her growing up and going out on her own.''

"But you haven't told her so, right?''

She nodded. From the four speakers, an Irish drinking song segued into a Newfoundland shipwreck ballad, and Keegan said, "And when the time comes, you'll let her go without a word, right?''

From the corner of his eye, he saw her funny little half smile and was shaken by a surge of spontaneous tenderness.

"Rich, what did your mother think when you joined the air force?''

"That I'd forget to take my vitamins and catch my death of cold because I never remembered to wear a sweater under my coat.''

"Those are a mother's code words,'' Maudie said, and Keegan thought he detected a teasing note in her husky voice.

"Code for what?''

"She was telling you how much she loved you, how much she was going to miss you—how lonesome she was going to be not having you there to look after. Having you all grown up so that you didn't need her any longer. Mothers need to be needed.''

"Everyone needs to be needed—by someone," he said quietly. They drove several miles in silence.

Maudie was grateful for the silence. Perhaps for the first time in her life, she realized that it was true. She realized, too, that it had been a mistake to let Rich drive her. Now she really *did* need him. If she had borrowed her father's pickup, or even Janine's car, she would have been completely independent.

How many years had she prided herself on her independence? The trouble with independence was that it didn't add up to security. Maybe nothing did. And the seclusion she had once sought—when had it turned from privacy into isolation? When had isolation turned into loneliness?

Turn your back and everything you believe in changes, she thought.

"Penny for them," Keegan offered. They were crossing the bridge over Oregon Inlet, a bridge that linked two fragile barrier islands together.

Maudie sighed, watching the swift currents eddying between the ever-shifting shoals that made the passage so treacherous. "I was thinking about independence. And security. And seclusion."

He nodded. "I've tried seclusion. Believe me, it's not what it's cracked up to be."

"You were hospitalized for your back, weren't you?"

Keegan nodded. By the time they rolled onto Bodie Island, he found himself telling her things he had never told anyone, not even his brothers, about a time when he hadn't known whether or not he would live to draw his next breath.

"How did it happen?" she asked.

"Fast. Too damn fast to do anything about it, even if I'd had any choice in the matter. Talk about being in the wrong place at the wrong time," he said in a self-deprecating tone that was distinctly different from his usual incisiveness. "I picked the middle of a damned Iraqi convoy to land in when I popped the tab."

"But you were rescued. I mean, you're here."

"Yeah. I was rescued." The Jolly Green Giant would have had him out of there before the silk settled except for a run of bad luck. "If I'd ejected about thirty seconds on either side of that damned Iraqi convoy, I'd have probably made it home a hell of a lot quicker, but I thought I had a good shot at getting back to base. You don't just throw away a piece of equipment like that if there's a chance to salvage it."

Maudie, who had salvaged herself a home from the ruins of another man's castle, nodded understandingly.

"My luck just ran out, that's all. I took a hit that jammed my radar. I might still have made it back, but too many systems started shutting down. It costs damned near as much to train a man to fly one of those babies as it does to build a replacement. So I got out."

"In the wrong place."

"Right. Honey, you don't want to hear about the life and times of a broken-down jet jockey. How about it, want some coffee? Need a pit stop?"

She nodded. What she needed was to find a pay phone and call the hospital. She had her wallet out before they even pulled up at the pumps, checking her change purse.

While Maudie went inside to get change, Keegan used his credit card and placed the call. Just in case the news was bad and he needed to act as a filter. By the time she got back, he was waiting with the good news.

The relatively good news. "I got through to Ann Mary's floor, thought you might like the latest report. Great news!"

"Dammit, Rich, I wanted to do it!"

"Ah, jeez, honey, I'm sorry. I should have thought of that, but I just figured I could save us some time by placing the call while you were getting your coffee."

Maudie stared down at the roll of quarters in her hand. She hadn't given coffee a second thought once she'd seen the phone. "You should have waited and let me talk to them," she muttered.

"Yeah. I keep putting my foot in it, don't I?"

"Well, what did they say? Did you talk to Ann Mary?" She braced herself visibly, and Keegan fought the urge to gather her into his arms and protect her against the world. She was so damned small, so damned vulnerable—and trying so damned hard not to show it.

In a ludicrous falsetto, he said, "Patient Ann Winters is doing as well as can be expected, and is being held over for observation." But at the look of imminent panic on her face, he dropped the clown act. "Hey, that's SOP, honey. It's the hospital's way of protecting against lawsuits, that's all."

"I know that. And they would have said—I mean, if there was anything really serious, they would have..." She swallowed visibly. "You told her I was coming, didn't you?"

"I told the nurse I was calling for Miss Winters's mother, and that we'd be there within two hours, max, and to pass it on."

This time he did draw her close, and Maudie leaned her forehead against Keegan's chest for just an instant. "What would I do without you?" she whispered against the solid wall of security he offered.

But she didn't want to think about that. Not now.

She was in a private room. Maudie didn't bat an eye. If she had to ransom her entire future, nothing mattered but that her baby was all right.

They hurried to the elevators. Maudie repeated the room number like a mantra while Keegan steered her through the crowd and along the corridor until he homed in on his target. "Just past the dressing cart on the left. You go ahead, honey, I'll be waiting at the end of the hall. If you need me for anything, just say the word, all right?"

Maudie could only nod. Later she would worry about all the things she didn't have time to worry about now. Lifting her head to thank him, she ran head-on into a quick, tender kiss that for one weak moment made her want to crawl back into his sheltering arms and hide.

"God bless," he whispered, and turning her, he patted her on her tick bite and shoved her through the partially closed door.

The first thing Maudie noticed was the black eye. The second was the cast on her daughter's right arm. The third was the skinny, bespectacled young man hovering over her bed.

A doctor? Wearing a sweatshirt that said For Details, See Bumper Sticker? Blushing hot enough to melt his plastic frames while he tried to pretend he hadn't been kissing her daughter when Maudie had walked through the door?

Whoa.

"Mama! Oh, Mama, you didn't have to—I told Jerry to tell you not to—"

"Baby, what happened?" Maudie hurriedly examined her child for signs of further damage. "Your poor face—and your arm! Are you all right? No, of course you're not all right! What happened? Tell me everything, and don't leave any of it out, because I'll hear it all from your doctor, so you may as well tell me."

"Mama, this is Leonard Stevens. We're engaged."

"Oh, God." Maudie sank onto the chair the young man shoved under her just in time. Her knees were wobbling, possibly because she had refused to let Keegan stop for food. She hadn't eaten all day.

Or possibly because she had seen her daughter only three weeks earlier, during Christmas break, and she had still been her baby then—a child who stirred her cocoa with peppermint sticks and wore bunny slippers and twirled the ends of her ponytail around her finger when she concentrated.

"Mama, I'm fine, honest. I've just got this broken arm in two places—that is, it's broken in two places—and Leo says my eye's really gross."

"I never said that, I said it was—"

"A classic shiner, but we both know what you meant," Ann Mary teased, pinching her battered lips to keep from grinning. "You did, too. You know you did."

"Well, what's wrong with that? You're going to see it. No point in my trying to shield you from the truth."

And the truth was, Maudie thought with greatly mixed feelings, she was about as welcome around here as a head cold.

"Mama, you didn't have to come. We only called you because Leo thought you'd want to know, but it's no big deal. I've got a few bruises and scratches, but other than that, I'm just fine. I'll probably go home tomorrow."

"Home?" Maudie repeated.

"Leo wants me to go stay with his mother. They live not far from campus, and he'll take me to classes. Mrs. Stevens says it's okay with her."

Maudie leaned back in her chair, feeling the way she'd felt the first time she'd stepped onto an escalator. Things were moving too fast. Things that weren't supposed to move at all. This was *her* baby, not Leo's. And certainly not some strange woman's who lived near the campus and said it was okay with her.

"Maudie?" It was Keegan.

Three faces turned toward the door. Maudie wanted to run and hide in his arms until her world settled down again. Instead she smiled and invited him inside. "Rich, this is my daughter, Ann Mary, and her friend, Leonard Stevens."

"Fiancé," Ann Mary corrected, and Keegan lifted his brows.

"Children—" Ann Mary would kill her for that, and Maudie couldn't much blame her, but dammit, they *were* children! "This is Colonel Keegan. He was kind enough to drive me here when the call came through."

She could see the curiosity spark her daughter's eyes, and she refused to satisfy it. What could she say? Colonel Keegan is the man with whom I happened to have been living for the past week and a half—the man I made love to three times last night? The man who taught me more about my own sexuality in one night than I managed to learn over thirty-eight years as a virgin, a wife and a divorcée?

"Miss Winters." Keegan smiled, and Maudie watched the curiosity on her daughter's face flicker and change into something more speculative.

"Stevens, glad to meet you. My congratulations and best wishes to you both. How did it happen?" And then he grinned that special grin of his, disarming them all, Maudie included, unfortunately. "The damage, I mean," he explained, "not the engagement."

Ten

Some baby, Keegan thought as he handed his keys to the parking attendant and led Maudie into the lobby of the hotel. Maudie's baby was a good five feet ten and weighed in at roughly half again what her mother did.

Shaking his head, he grinned. Here he'd been picturing a cuddly, bright-eyed kid with—if she was lucky—some hint of one day possessing a portion of Maudie's serene beauty. And if she was luckier still, Maudie's strength of character.

Instead he'd been greeted by a black-haired Amazon with a battered grin cram full of her own brand of impudence.

"Some baby you've got there, honey," he said as they approached the black marble desk. Before Maudie could open her mouth to speak to the desk clerk, Keegan cut her off. "I'll handle it."

"Thank you, but I'm perfectly capable of booking myself a room."

"Humor me, will you? It's been a long day and my hand hurts like hell." Which was no more than the truth, but ordinarily he wouldn't have laid a guilt trip on her. Right now that would be hitting below the belt.

But, hey—who ever said a man had to play fair? "A double, please. Seventh floor or below, and could you throw in a Jacuzzi?"

"Separate rooms, any floor, and I'm paying for mine," Maudie countered.

"Fire ladders don't reach above the seventh."

"Then quit playing with matches."

"She's just tired," he explained to the elderly clerk, who nodded patiently. No doubt he had seen and heard it all before.

They settled for a double suite, and Keegan led her across the carpeted lobby to the bank of elevators, carrying both bags in his good hand. He could read her like a neon sign. She was running on fumes. One spark was all it would take.

Priority one: food. Priority two: a nice, relaxing bath—all of the above to be served with sufficient wine to complete the process. After that, they could talk.

Right. And after that he could begin to sort out a few of the problems that were beginning to jam his own internal radar.

Keegan dumped both bags at the foot of the king-size bed. Maudie scooped up her own and headed for the connecting door.

He followed her. "Hang around a few minutes, will you? I might need you," he said, holding up his injured hand.

"Oh, Lord, I forgot. Here, let me see. Why didn't you remind me while we were at the hospital? We could have had someone—here, come into the bathroom, maybe there's—take off your coat. I don't suppose you thought to bring along the—"

It had taken him a week to learn that when she was strung out emotionally, which wasn't often, she finished about one out of every three sentences. He liked the feeling of knowing her so well.

Liked it a little too much. "Maudie."

"Here you've been driving all day with your poor hand, and even before that, I—"

"Maudie."

In the middle of scrambling through a basket of amenities, as if she expected to find a first-aid kit nestled among the shampoo, lotion, shower cap and mouthwash, she glanced over her shoulder, and he saw the exhaustion in her eyes and the droop at the corners of her mouth. Her skin was the color of bleached bone.

"Come on, honey, it'll keep. I'll check out the pharmacy across the street if you'll dive into the Jacuzzi and stay there until I get back."

She started to protest, but he laid a finger across her lips. On second thought, he leaned down and replaced it with his own lips.

As a kiss, it was slow to kindle. They were both tired, and Maudie's worries had refocused and dug in. Lifting the gentle pressure of his mouth, Keegan reminded himself that all they had eaten for the past dozen or so hours was vending machine junk. No fuel, no energy.

"Tell you what, let's order up dinner first, and then you climb into the tub while I go across the street. We'll eat, and then we'll call the hospital and you can say good-night to your baby."

Maudie blinked twice at that broad, steady chest, those strong, comforting arms. Sighing, she surrendered a fraction of an inch of ground. "I suppose we do have to eat."

"I suppose you're right," he teased, and was gratified to see an answering gleam in her shadowed green eyes. "So get moving, woman, and while you're shedding your clothes you can tell me how you like your steak cooked."

"See what kind of pasta they offer, will you?"

"Medium or rare? You can have pasta for breakfast. Right now you need some good class-A protein."

"I don't feel like eating red meat tonight."

"Right. One rare, one well done, trim the fat on both. That suit you?"

"You always think you know what's good for everybody. See if they have broiled chicken."

"Not always. If I ever make a mistake, I'll be the first to admit it, I promise you."

"I want a front row seat for that." She flexed her shoulders tiredly. "Rich—what did you think of her? Isn't she lovely? She has a straight A average, and she's carrying a jillion hours with all those 'osophies and 'ologies she dotes on."

"Looks to me like that's not all she dotes on."

Dropping onto a chair, Maudie toed off her shoes. "Yes, well. I intend to talk to her about that tomorrow. She's still just a baby."

"How old were you when she was born?"

"That's beside the point."

"Uh-huh." He smiled. Stepping back into the bathroom, he turned on both faucets full blast and adjusted the temperature. "I sort of expected your baby to look more like you," he called through the door. "She must take after her father."

Massaging her scalp, which felt about two sizes too small at the moment, Maudie said, "In looks, maybe, but that's all. She's really nothing at all like Sanford except for her height and her coloring. Ann Mary's sweet and patient and kind. She's always had a wonderful sense of humor, even as a child."

Which told him a lot about her ex. Keegan stashed the knowledge away in a mental file labeled Maudie: What Makes Her Tick. From the bathroom, he dialed room service and ordered two steak dinners, both medium rare, with baked potatoes, tossed salads, oil and vinegar with Parmesan on the side, and a bottle of their best cabernet Sauvignon.

From the doorway, Maudie glared at him. "If you're finished, I'll call and order *my* dinner now. I'm going to have—"

"I just did."

"—broiled chicken breast with rice and steamed vegetables, and ice cream and coffee, and—and maybe coconut pie if they have it."

"We'll check out the desserts after we finish our steaks. Otherwise the pie'll be cold and the ice cream melted."

"That means two trips and two tips! Dammit, Keegan, I—"

"My treat. I need a little pampering tonight, so humor me, will you?"

"Keegan, I don't care how much you throw your weight around on your own territory, I don't happen to be one of your soldiers! Now, give me that phone."

"Technically, they're airmen. The bathtub's filling fast if you want to fine tune the temperature."

"I don't care if they're dodo birds! You—"

"I guess you noticed there's plenty of room for two people in there if you need a lifeguard."

Growling deep in her throat, she lunged past him and slammed the bathroom door shut. She was flat out of patience or she would have marched downstairs and demanded a single room on the opposite side of the building.

On the opposite side of the planet!

Unfortunately, if there was one thing Maudie was a real sucker for, it was a tub bath. It had been nearly two years since she had enjoyed the luxury of her father's old clawfooted bathtub.

Prowling the room, Keegan opened the draperies and stared down at the city lights. Was he pushing too hard? He had deliberately kept the pressure on, knowing instinctively that anger might just keep her from collapsing into bed on an empty stomach with her muscles all tied into knots.

With Maudie, it was hard to tell when enough was too much. She was a low pressure kind of woman with more strength than was immediately evident. Something had kept her putting one foot in front of the other for the past twenty-odd years without any evidence of the bitterness or desperation he had seen in other women in her circumstances.

He wanted to give her—

Hell, he didn't know what he wanted to give her. A lot more than she wanted to accept, he'd be willing to bet. It was going to be tricky, working around that devilish pride of hers.

Chicken and rice. Had she forgotten telling him that she didn't care for chicken? She probably didn't even like rice.

As for the pie, he would see that she got it if he had to go to Tahiti for coconuts and then bake the thing himself.

"I'm off to the pharmacy. Anything you need before I go?" he called through the door.

"No, thank you."

Meek as a spring lamb. Which probably meant she was working up a good head of steam. "You're sure, now? Powder? Potato chips? Panty hose?" He didn't want her falling asleep in there before he got back.

"Would you please go fight a war or something and leave me alone? Argh!"

Grinning broadly, Keegan scooped up the things he wanted cleaned and laundered, saluted the closed bathroom door, and left.

The steaks were overcooked, the potatoes mushy, and the salad unimaginative, but they were both too hungry to complain.

Maudie tore open a roll and slathered it with butter. "Chicken would've been better."

"You don't like chicken, remember?"

"What makes you think—?" She shook her head. "You know, you're a royal pain when it comes to getting your own way."

Keegan topped off their wineglasses. They were seated at the table. He had rather pictured them eating in bed, but then his fantasies had always had touch of Tom Jones about them. "That's what people keep telling me. Funny, I never saw it that way."

"You wouldn't. Tell me about your family, Rich. How do they manage to put up with your king-of-the-world attitude?"

"Beats me," he said simply. And then he shrugged. "Matter of fact, that's why I showed up on your doorstep. After they'd had a bellyful of having their lives micro-managed, they delegated a spokesman to suggest that I go south for the sake of my health. At least, I thought it was my health they were thinking about, not their own." Toying with a button on his sleeve that was hanging by a thread, he laughed, but the laughter never quite reached his eyes.

After a while, Maudie said, "You're serious, aren't you?"

"Nah, I'm kidding."

"You're serious. Rich, you're their brother. Brothers are entitled to meddle."

"My baby sister is only a year older than Ann Mary. She—"

"She needs you."

"As I was saying, she's an anthropology student, married to another anthropology student. The two of them, along with a dozen or so other students, spend their summers digging holes in the ground with teaspoons. They're so wrapped up in each other and what they're doing they haven't even noticed I'm back from the war."

Her eyes widened. "Oh, no—I know that's not true."

"Okay, so I exaggerated a bit for effect. The point I'm trying to make, honey, is that people generally grow up and make new lives for themselves, and when they do, other relationships have to change. Not end, mind you—but change. Definitely. It's called growth, and if we're lucky, we all do it."

"But you—"

"Hey, don't get the wrong idea. I'm still a big brother. I'll always be that, just like Ann Mary will always be your daughter, but the kids don't need us any longer to cut their meat for them and tell them when to wear their raincoats. They're adults. They're busy building families of their own. Mine have already built 'em."

"Ann Mary's still just a baby, but Rich, you—"

Reaching across the table, Keegan wiped a smear of butter from Maudie's lips with his thumb. "Don't sweat it, sweetheart. Things have a way of working out. It's not what happens to you so much as it is your attitude toward what happens.''

Somewhat to her own surprise, Maudie wasn't nearly as concerned with her daughter's latest fancy as she was with Rich's uncaring family. To heck with attitudes! He had been their big brother all his life, and she knew as well as she knew her own name that he would never have shirked or resented a single one of his responsibilities. He was that kind of man.

She would give a front tooth to have his battalion of unappreciative siblings lined up in front of her for just five minutes. She could tell them a thing or two about just how rare a man like Richmond Keegan really was! A truly caring man. A kind man and—all right, an aggravating man!

But even that was only because he genuinely thought he knew best and was determined to do whatever had to be done, even if he hurt himself in the process.

Such as driving her to the hospital with his injured hand instead of letting her set out alone in her father's pickup. She had argued at the time that he would probably want to keep on heading north once he got that far instead of having to turn around and drive her back home, but he'd told her not to worry about it, and her father had offered to come pick her up, and Rich had told him he would call if they needed him to make the trip.

Maudie hadn't wanted to think about it at the time. She still didn't.

He had hung around, though. Hung around long enough to get her out of Ann Mary's room before she said something she would regret about that so-called engagement. Fiancé! Good Lord, Ann Mary was barely out of braces!

"Rich, how old were you when you got married?" she asked suddenly.

Keegan choked on his coffee. "How—? Uh, let's see—
I guess I was about twenty-seven, maybe twenty-eight. Old
enough to have known better."

"What happened?"

"Honey, you don't want to dig into my boring past
again. We've been through that. If I thought it would help
any, I'd be glad to tell you anything you want to know, but
Alice and I are history."

"They say if you don't learn from history, you'll repeat
the same mistakes over and over."

"You mean me?"

"No, I mean me. Actually, I mean Ann Mary."

He blew out his breath in a long stream. "Okay, you
asked for it. Alice was originally from Stamford. We were
introduced by one of my sisters. She's tall, slim, bru-
nette—physically one of the most beautiful women I've
ever known. She's intelligent. She's lazy. We both liked
flying, we both liked sports cars, we both liked s— Uh,
well we had a lot in common. Or so it seemed at the time."

Maudie's spirits dragged bottom. She told herself it had
been a long day and knew it was far more than that. Had
she truly expected Rich to have married a homely woman
who enjoyed looking after indigent racoons and watching
the weather change? "So what happened?"

"Not a whole lot. We got married while I was home on
leave from Davis-Monthan AFB. I got sent overseas about
the time Alice was offered a job as a TV spokes model on
a Tucson station. Naturally, she wasn't eager to leave, so
we sort of commuted." And in between commutes, he had
learned later, his wife had played house with anything in
pants who offered her a little excitement. "In time, we
discovered that we weren't particularly interested in the
same things any longer. When she asked for a divorce, I

didn't have any objections." Oversimplification number three-hundred twenty-seven.

Maudie stirred the third spoonful of sugar in her coffee. And stirred and stirred, until Rich reached across the table and removed the teaspoon from her hand. She smiled, and he smiled back. A feeling of—of *something*—passed between them, yet neither of them dared to examine it too closely.

"What about your guy?" he asked after she had sampled her coffee, grimaced, and set the cup back into its saucer.

"His name is Sanford. I heard last year that he's now a board certified specialist. Plastic surgery." She smiled again, and this time, it sparkled from her eyes. "I don't know why I should be surprised at his choice."

"No night calls?"

"That, too. But mostly I guess it's because he was always so good at manipulating people. Making them into what he wanted them to be, and then changing them again on a whim. Or trying to."

"Why'd you marry him?"

"He asked me. I was so impressed with his looks, his manners—everything—but mostly because I didn't know any better. San thought I was land rich because I mentioned this tract of land my family owned on the Outer Banks, and told him all about this island we owned half of, and the rich yankee sportsman who had built this fabulous club there back in early part of the century. I think he had visions of getting together a partnership and developing every square inch into high-rise condominiums."

Keegan laughed. "This is Coronoke Island we're talking about?"

"And Hatteras. All this was before even the most rudimentary zoning was put into place, remember. Sanford had seen what was being done north of the inlet and thought he could make a killing by moving south a few miles and picking up whatever the Park Service didn't own.''

"Nice dream.''

"Not very realistic.''

"My great-grandfather did it.''

"On a limited basis, and only for ninety-nine years.'' Keegan frowned slightly, but Maudie didn't notice. "Besides, it was probably good for the economy back then. Granddaddy wasn't the only one who made enough off guiding and caretaking to build himself a house with indoor plumbing. The developers hadn't made a meal of the place back then.''

Keegan pushed back from the table and held out his hand. "Want to take a run around the block to work off some of our dinner?''

As they were both dressed in the hotel's voluminous terry-cloth bathrobes, the suggestion was largely rhetorical. "What I really want to do is call the hospital and then sleep for eight hours without moving a muscle. If it's all the same to you, I'll just dream I'm jogging a few miles.''

While Maudie called the hospital, Keegan cleared away the remains of their meal, set the tray outside, and as she was still talking when he finished that, he unpacked her overnight bag, hanging her few things in the capacious closet. His own were already in the process of being laundered and dry-cleaned, and would be delivered to the room before breakfast. Otherwise he was going to be at a pretty large disadvantage.

"She says she's being discharged tomorrow as soon as her doctor makes his rounds,'' Maudie said as she hung up the phone.

"Good.''

"Which is more or less what she said earlier."

Keegan watched her closely. Her hands, which had been quieter than usual all day, were lying limp in her lap, and on impulse he crossed to her toilet case and removed her hairbrush. Using the hotel's shampoo, which was okay, but it didn't smell like clover, she had washed her hair earlier. It hung untended around her tired face.

Keegan felt a few more blocks in the fortress he had erected around his heart a long time ago begin to crumble.

"Lean over, you don't want to sleep with rats' nests in your hair," he murmured, drawing the brush through her shoulder-length, leaf-brown hair. "I used to do this for my baby sister and then braid it before we went to church. Otherwise she'd probably still be a heathen. Mother refused to let us out of the house unless we all passed inspection."

Maudie pictured him as a boy, big for his age, overly serious as he shouldered the responsibility for an ailing, widowed mother. She wished he had been her brother.

Oh, no she didn't!

"Have you figured out tomorrow yet?" he asked her as he drew the brush slowly out from her scalp.

"I haven't even figured out tonight," she said, and then blushed. "I didn't say that, and you didn't hear it."

He grinned and kept on brushing, his left hand nearly as dextrous as his right.

She didn't want to sleep alone. Yet how could she risk getting any more involved than she already was? Twenty-four hours ago she hadn't been quite sure. Now she was, and the pain eclipsed even the pain of knowing she was losing her daughter to some wet-necked puppy with an overbite and a taste for droll sweatshirts.

As if he had read her mind, Keegan said, "Honey, it's been a long day and we're both pretty strung out. I'll level with you—I don't think you're ready for any more excitement, and I doubt if I'm up to generating any."

Maudie hid her disappointment behind a suspiciously brilliant smile.

And then he said, "On the other hand, I don't think either one of us particularly feels like being alone tonight. So how about we spoon up and let it go at that? I don't mind telling you that I still have a few nightmares about my hitch in solitary—mostly when I've pushed too hard. I could use a warm body in the night, just to remind me that I'm back among the living again."

She had forgotten. All she had done was take, and all he had done was give. Less than a week ago he had still been suffering from a war injury—Lord knows what emotional injuries he had suffered! And here she was letting him take on her care and feeding just as if he owed it to her.

"I'd like that," she admitted.

She must have imagined the quick flare of intensity that lit his eyes for an instant. He was as tired as she was. He'd said so. She watched as he replaced her hairbrush on the dresser and turned off the bedside lamp, leaving a narrow sliver of light to spill in from the other room. It occurred to her to wonder if he ever slept in complete darkness.

The lighted candle had been so that he wouldn't trip if he had to get up in the night. She had accepted it as perfectly logical, but perhaps there was more to it than that.

Perhaps there was something she could offer him, after all. If only for a little while.

Eleven

Warmth. Reaching out in the dark and finding warmth instead of the slick cold surface of an unused pillow. Maudie awoke with the indescribable feeling of having been held and loved through the night, even though Keegan had been asleep almost as soon as he closed his eyes.

"Ready for dessert?" he murmured, stirring warm currents of air against her left ear.

"Now?" The curtains were drawn, the light still spilling across the carpeted floor from the other room. She had no way of knowing what time it **was**.

"I could send out a scouting party in search of coconut pie, or..."

"Or?" Her heart expanded, yet her chest felt suddenly hollow. The last thing she needed now was one more memory to add to her precious small heap. She had already collected far too many.

"Your choice," he said, his hands already creating memories that would last far too long in a bleak and empty future.

"Ah, Keegan, don't do this to me," Maudie groaned, turning in his arms. But it was already too late, and they both knew it. Why was he even offering her the choice? He never asked—he simply acted.

The intimacy alone would have defeated her, but then he had to go and lick that sensitive place between her neck and her shoulder that drove her wild. He had discovered it the night before—or was it the night before the night before?

Maudie was losing track of time. Had there ever been a period in her life when Keegan was not at the center of it?

"Oh, please," she whimpered as his mouth moved down the slope of her breast. Lightning streaked through her, stabbing again and again between her thighs. She clutched at his shoulders, her fingers digging into the hard, resilient muscles. He was a hard and resilient man, and she, God help her, was anything but! Today or tomorrow or the next day, he would move on and never look back, leaving her to her barren self-sufficiency.

Leaving her.

Powerless to resist, Maudie closed her eyes and surrendered to the inevitable. Keegan loved her with an exquisite tenderness that tore the heart right out of her. No part of her body went unloved. How long they lay in that big tumbled bed, she had no way of knowing. She only knew that by the time he positioned himself above her, she was one vast, aching, throbbing, disaster area!

This time he had protection, but nothing from any pharmacy could protect her heart. That was already lost. Cupping her face between his unsteady hands, Keegan held her soul captive with the sheer intensity of his October-blue eyes while he proceeded to conquer her body.

In an hour, or a day, or a week he'd be gone, Maudie told herself as, fathoms deep in love, she forgot the past, forgot the future, and gave herself to the moment. She gasped as he filled her, gasped once more as he slid his hands beneath her back and lifted her up to sit astride his thighs.

"Don't move," he grated, burying his face in her throat. His breath was harsh against the early morning stillness. His hands dug almost painfully into her hips, holding her still when she wanted desperately to give in to the maddening urge to twist and writhe against him.

"Rich, please, I—"

"Ah, Maudie, you don't know how much I—"

His ragged words covered hers, and she leaned back in his arms, holding her breath as she searched his face.

That small movement was all it took to trigger the avalanche, and heedless of danger, they rode the crest, hurtling breathlessly into oblivion.

Eons later, the phone buzzed discreetly on the table beside the bed. Keegan twisted around and reached for it.

"Watch your back," Maudie warned, trying to free herself from a tangle of limbs and bed linen.

"Wake up call," Keegan muttered. "Go back to sleep while I shower and shave." He responded with the room number, listened a moment, nodded, and then handed the phone to Maudie. "Sorry. Your daughter," he said. "She wants to talk to you."

Maudie closed her eyes and groaned. "Oh, Lord, how'm I ever going to explain th— Hello, baby, are you all right? You're sure?"

There was a long pause, during which Keegan could hear the tinny sound of a voice on the other end. "Half-past nine!" Maudie exclaimed. "What time is it now? But, honey, I wanted to—"

Keegan listened as she made half a dozen attempts to protest whatever was happening. He hadn't helped matters by answering the phone. One of these days he might learn to quit automatically taking charge of every situation.

Then, again, he might not.

"You stay right where you are, you hear me? We'll be there in—Rich, how long does it take to get to the hospital?" And then she tied it up in ribbons by saying, "No, we haven't had breakfast yet, but that can wait. Ann Mary, I don't want you to leave until I get there, you hear? I don't even know these people you're wanting to go home with!"

She hung up quickly before her daughter could protest again, and Keegan wondered how he'd ever been fooled into thinking his Maudie was cool, calm and collected.

His Maudie?

Yeah. His Maudie. If he had anything at all to say about the situation. And with a few notable exceptions, he usually managed to have quite a lot to say about any situation.

Unfed, but hastily showered and dressed, they were halfway to the hospital when Maudie's brain caught up with her mouth. "Oh, no," she wailed.

Keegan braked behind a delivery truck that blocked the stoplight overhead. He felt like pulling her into his arms and telling her to forget it—that her little girl was a big girl, and Maudie had her own life to live.

But if he got started on that subject, they'd never get there in time. "Don't sweat it, Maudie. Two more lights and then hang a left—right?"

"How could you let me make such a complete idiot of myself?" she demanded.

"You want to be more specific?"

"You know what I mean!"

"So I answered the phone. It's no big deal. Ann Mary knows I'm chauffeuring you around."

"Yes, but I even admitted to her that we hadn't had breakfast yet, which was as good as admitting that—"

"That we haven't had breakfast yet. Don't sweat it, Maudie. Ann Mary strikes me as a pretty savvy little lady."

"That's just what I'm afraid of!"

Keegan turned into the already crowded parking lot just as a slot on the front row was vacated. Without questioning his luck, he pulled in, switched off the engine and set the brake. Turning, he said, "Listen to me, Maudie Winters, we're going in there together and your daughter can think whatever she wants to think. If her guy is with her, so much the better."

"How can you—"

"Because your baby's a grown woman, and the sooner you face that fact, the sooner you'll both be able to enjoy a different kind of relationship."

"I don't *want* a different kind of relationship!"

"No, honey, I don't suppose you do. We all want to think that we can hang on to whatever gives purpose and meaning to our lives, but we're not living in one of those pretty little snowball paperweights with a neat little house that never needs repainting and a neat little tree that never needs trimming or fertilizing."

Maudie's eyes were shadowed with concern, but she had to laugh at that. "You're not exactly describing my life-style, in case you hadn't noticed."

"Yeah, well...we'll talk about your life-style later. Right now, you need to know something I finally figured out while I was flat on my back on a door, wondering when the roof was going to cave in on my head."

"The roof is perfectly sound in that part of the house, or else I'd never have—"

"Right. Like I said, later. Meanwhile, Keegan's en-
lightenment, clause two, item one, says that life's a moving target. You move with it, or you lose it."

"Keegan, my daughter is waiting to be discharged from
the hospital. Either give me the condensed version or can
it, will you?"

"Right. Short version. Families have a way of growing
up when we aren't looking. Like it or not, they're hellbent
on living their own lives. Mothers and big brothers can either be a part of those changing lives or we can drop out.
The one thing we can't do is keep everything the way it was
yesterday. That's the gist of Keegan's Philosophy 101 on
interfamily relationships."

She was still staring at him, seemingly lost in space,
when he said briskly, "Now, I vote we go find your
daughter and any friends she happens to be attached to
and take 'em out to breakfast. You can butter her toast if
it'll make you feel better. She'll probably even let you get
away with it. This time."

Maudie was largely silent on the drive home. It had
rained part of the way, a cold, cheerless drizzle that promised hazardous driving if the temperatures fell another few
degrees, but once they neared the narrow strip of barrier
island leading south from Oregon Inlet, it was at least ten
degrees warmer, if no less dismal.

Keegan juggled defrost and windshield wipers, and as
they passed the stoic old Life Saving Station at Chicami-
comico, he switched on a CD. Irish music from Newfoundland flowed from the four speakers, something slow
and haunting about a shipwreck. Appropriate, he thought,
for another misplaced Irishman, several generations removed. He thought some more about the various quirks of
fate that could send a man around the world time and
again and then dump him on an island hundreds of miles

away from his home and give him not only the urge, but the means, to begin putting down fresh roots.

"What you told Ann Mary—is that true?" Maudie asked. She'd been quiet for so long she might have been napping, but Keegan had sensed that she was awake. In the marrow of his bones, where his personal truths resonated, he had followed her thoughts as they drove south after leaving the Stevenses and Ann Mary in the hospital parking lot.

He mumbled something about his plans to restore the Hunt if the family expert deemed it feasible, and if he could come to terms with her father, but his mind was not on his plans for the future—at least not those particular plans. Because it had come to him slowly over the past twenty-four hours that he could no longer conceive of a future that didn't include this woman.

This small, composed, passionate, determined woman, who, more than any woman he had ever met, had a strength and beauty that was soul deep. "Like I said," he murmured, "it depends."

"But why? It's not as if you were a developer or even a builder. Besides, your family's all up in Connecticut. So why?"

He considered his words carefully. The smart thing would be to wait about a week. A day, at least. She was looking far too fragile, and while he accepted responsibility for the shadows around her eyes—she hadn't had a whole lot of sleep lately; would have had far less if he'd had his way—Keegan refused to take responsibility for her sagging spirits. Those had come with the realization that her baby was all grown up and was never going to need her mama in quite the same way again.

But, dammit, *he* needed her! Why couldn't that be enough for her? It wasn't the same. He could never take the place of her daughter. That was the last thing he would want to do! But wasn't there a little room in her life for a man who loved her passionately, who needed her desperately, who wanted to give her the world tied up in silver ribbons?

Or at least a solid roof over her head.

They'd had breakfast at a cafeteria near the hospital. Keegan had more or less ramrodded the whole affair. He had talked to Ann Mary's young man, discreetly sounding out his prospects, while Maudie had made polite conversation with Mrs. Stevens. Ann Mary had buttered her own toast, thank you very much. No help needed.

Over second cups of coffee, the tableau had shifted. Mrs. Stevens had gone to powder her nose and Keegan had talked to Ann Mary while the Stevens kid had tried valiantly to engage Maudie in a discussion of the future possibilities of a newly graduated geology major who had inherited a bundle of stock in a mine somewhere out in Utah.

Poor Maudie. She had tried her best to be cheerful but her hands hadn't moved from her lap once since she'd shoved her untouched plate aside. Her fixed smile had cracked his heart wide open and left it bleeding. All in the world he'd wanted by then was to get her out of there, to get her back to her island where he could convince her that she wasn't alone, and that he wasn't such a bad bargain.

But first he had to convince himself.

After all she'd been through in the past twenty-four hours, Keegan knew he would be a fool to barge ahead now. It was going to take more than finesse to convince any woman in her right mind to take on a man with nothing more tangible than a headful of crazy ideas about an island inn complete with air taxi service. A man with a back that had been torn and mended once too often. A man who was set in his ways and who possessed, according to his own sisters, who loved him in spite of it, a streak of male chauvinism five miles wide.

Good intentions didn't count. Timing was all important, which meant he'd better stick to practical matters and leave the tricky stuff for later.

"About the Hunt," he said. "I checked it out pretty thoroughly. It's in better shape than I thought. Some of it's already gone, some's on the way out, but I was thinking if we start small, maybe clear away both wings and rebuild the central back portion, add on a decent kitchen, a couple more bedrooms and some functioning indoor plumbing, maybe later on extend an all-weather room out over the sound..."

"Excuse me, but who's going to look after this empire you're planning on building?"

Here was his chance. "I thought we, uh, we can talk details later. I just wanted to know what you thought about the basics."

"It doesn't really matter what I think. You'll do as you please. You always do, don't you?"

After a while, he said very quietly, "No. Not always."

Keegan pulled in at the grocery store, and when Maudie started to get out, he shook his head. "Stay here. Grab a nap. I'll get whatever we need for the next few days."

For once, Maudie was tired enough to obey. Not to sleep, but at least to close her eyes. One small corner of her heart snatched at the hope he had hinted at, while a tired portion of her brain whispered, *He's just like Sanford.* Just let him meet a banker woman with a little bit of property and he sees a fortune in real estate falling into his hot, greedy little hands.

But Keegan was nothing like Sanford. Was he? She'd been burned once. She'd thought she had learned her lesson, but maybe there were some lessons no woman ever learned, not deep down in her heart.

Was it a universal truth that loving inevitably led to losing? If so, then she wished she'd been born in another universe.

It was nearly pitch dark by the time they untied the boat and set out for the island. The marina was closed for the night. Off season, it was only manned a few hours a day, and even those hours were subject to change without notice.

"You're too isolated out here," Keegan said as he guided them out past the breakwaters.

"It's called privacy. Some people prefer it."

"What do you do when all the cottages are rented?"

"Endure."

"The way you've had to endure my company?"

She caught her breath audibly over the roar of the outboard, and he stared through the dusk at her huddled figure. In the car, she had looked too pale, all except for the tip of her nose, which was too pink. His thirteen-year-old niece's nose always turned pink when she was trying to hold back tears.

God, how was it possible to feel another person's pain, to feel her joy, her laughter, her hopes and fears the way he felt Maudie's? Never in his entire life had he felt this close to another person. It was scary. He felt like a raw, inexperienced kid instead of a man who had been married once and had known more women than he could easily recall.

"So," he said, lifting his voice over the roar. "What if I wanted to book all five for a month, starting in about two weeks, give or take a few days?"

"All *five?*" Maudie gawked at him. He idled down and quartered the whitecaps, having learned by watching her. Even so, they were both getting drenched from spray, along with the drizzle that continued to fall. This was a hell of a time to bring it up. Why hadn't he waited until he got her home?

Ah, jeez! "Well, maybe just three. I thought Ken and his family, maybe Dennis and Mary and theirs, or Sara and Bill. Most of the kids are in school, but I thought maybe half a dozen or so of Ken's crew who could—"

"Rich, could you just concentrate on what you're doing and get us home before we drown? We can talk about whatever it is you've got on your mind once we get a fire going. I've never been so cold in my life."

"Right." Bracing the tiller with his knee, Keegan slipped off his leather jacket and spread it over Maudie's huddled shoulders, ignoring her protests. He might not be the world's most polished lover, but at least he could keep her from freezing.

By the time they got the fire going and the groceries hauled up from the boat and put away, Maudie had begun to thaw out. Under her instructions, Keegan adjusted the draft on the wood stove and added a chunk of ironwood to the split pine and dried oak. For a man who had once thought he knew all the answers, he was learning a lot about the basics of survival.

Keegan made the coffee and Maudie produced the brandy. Together, they made thick, untidy sandwiches and dragged their chairs closer to the fire. Outside, the rain beat against the windows. The old house creaked as heat began to spread to the ancient wooden walls.

"Surprising how quickly a man can get attached to living this way," he said after a while.

Maudie sipped her coffee appreciatively. It was one of the exotic blends Keegan had chosen. Let him loose in a grocery store and he would wreck her budget in the first five minutes, but she was determined to enjoy it while it lasted.

And him.

"Mmm," she murmured, her gaze moving over the long, muscular legs that stretched out to rest on the kindling basket.

"'Course, not many women would be satisfied to live in a place like this."

"Mmm." She warmed her cold hands on the hot mug, warning herself not to listen too closely, not to read too much into what he was saying. Not to hope.

"Like I said on the way over, I was thinking we could sort of start small and grow slowly. Nothing too drastic. Nothing Regina wouldn't approve of."

Behave yourself, heart! He's talking real estate, not romance! "I can book however many cottages you want if you'll give me the exact dates," she said calmly. "Your family might not like Coronoke. Some people want waterslides and bingo parlors with their beaches."

"They'll love it. Wait'll they see it in the summertime."

"You haven't even seen it in the summertime," she said dryly, admiring the way the lamplight delineated his craggy features, the soft, random growth of his hair. He wasn't suave. He wasn't handsome, not in the classic sense. He wasn't...perfect. And heaven help her, she loved him all the more for his flaws.

Impatient with her own weakness, she thumped her mug onto the table and frowned at him, shoving her hair back from her face. "Keegan, would you please just tell me what in the world this is all about? You're talking about a whole congregation, and February can be the bleakest, coldest, stormiest—! Besides which, I've already drained all the pipes and put antifreeze in the traps and the—"

"I don't suppose you'd be interested in marrying me, would you?"

"Toilet tanks and—"

"No, well—maybe you could just think about it a while and give me an answer later on, when you've rested up."

"What did you say?"

"It's not a congregation, it's just Ken's construction crew. Skeleton crew, at least. And some family. When I called from the hospital this morning, Ken said he thought he could pull together enough to size the job up and see what it'll take. I thought the family might like to get involved, seeing as how—"

"Yes."

"—it's part of the Keegan heritage. Benji—he's one of my nephews—he's got this chest condition. He's supposed to grow out of it, but the way they keep babying him, I dunno. Anyway, I thought—" He blinked. "Did you say yes?"

She nodded. "I'm not sure what the proper form is. Yes, sir? Yes, Colonel? How about, yes, indeedy?"

Keegan's eyes widened. Slowly, he sat up in the spraddled old wicker rocking chair and turned around. "Maudie? Did you just do what I thought you did?"

"Well, I'm not sure, now that you ask. It was all sort of mixed up with toilet tanks and carpenter crews. I got the impression you'd asked me to marry you, but I'd be the first to admit I might have heard wrong. If I did, you can—"

He was out of his chair before she could move, kneeling before her on the old scarred and water-stained oak floor. Maudie felt tears spring to her eyes at the sight of this big, battered warrior on his knees, but when she protested, Keegan laughed and said, "Believe me, it's safer than bending over. Sweetheart, are you sure you know what you're letting yourself in for?"

"No. But I'm willing to listen if you want to enlighten me."

"Where do I start?"

She wasn't about to prompt him. Either he said it of his own accord, or he didn't say it at all. And if he didn't, why then, she would probably marry him, anyway, if he wanted her. Which only proved what she had suspected, that there are some lessons a woman never learns.

His hands rested on her thighs, his head was on a level with hers. Light from the forty-watt bulb glistened on the silver strands frosting his shaggy, dark blond crew cut. His eyes were shadowed with emotion, her own suspiciously moist.

"That's up to you," she said huskily.

"We could start with the fact that a broken-down ex-jet jockey probably doesn't have a whole lot in common with a young and beautiful woman who owns her own island."

He was nervous. Maudie's heart melted. The brash, arrogant officer, a man used to commanding men and machines, was sweating and swallowing visibly. "On the other hand," she said gently. "A middle-aged caretaker doesn't have a lot in common with a gentleman and an officer who's seen everything worth seeing and done everything worth doing."

"Irrelevant. What about love?" he ventured.

Maudie resisted touching the endearing cowlick—not the one on top, but the one where his hairline was beginning to recede. "There's that," she whispered. Waiting. Hardly daring to hope.

"I, uh, I do. You, that is. A lot. A hell of a lot. I, ah, jeez, this isn't sounding the way I wanted it to sound."

"How did you want it to sound?" Her heart was in her eyes. He had to know how she felt. Was he—could he possibly be—as uncertain of himself as she was?

With a ragged bark of laughter, he said, "Coherent would have helped. Maudie, God knows, I'm no bargain, but I don't think I can stand it if you don't love me, at least a little bit. Do you? Or if it's too soon, do you think maybe you could learn to?"

Maudie closed her eyes for fear her soul would fly right out into his arms. "Oh, yes," she crooned softly. "I do. So much I feel like I'm about to burst right wide open with all these crazy feelings. I don't know how it happened, but I do know it's more real than anything that's ever happened to me before."

With an exclamation that was half profane and half prayer, Keegan buried his face in her lap. And then he stood and drew her to her feet, grinning down at her from his superior height. "We've got a lot of plans to make, lady. I'm going to tangle you up in so much official red tape you won't stand a chance of escaping, not for the next fifty or so years."

"Fine," she said agreeably. The smile that had kindled in her eyes spread to her lips, and she gazed up at her big, rugged, imperfect warrior. "I'll leave all the planning to you, since you're so good at it. Tomorrow you can start making lists, but for now, don't you think we'd better get some rest?"

Keegan could no more hold back his truimphant grin than he could hold back the sunset. He swung her up into his arms, and Maudie cried, "Watch your back! Don't you dare hurt it now!"

"Don't worry, sweet pea, I've got plans for that back. What do you say we get started on the honeymoon before all our kinfolk descend on us?"

"That's what I like about you, Colonel. You're so darned efficient. My bed or yours?" Maudie teased, lifting her face for his kiss.

After a long while, Keegan murmured, "How about ours?"

*   *   *   *   *

Take 4 bestselling love stories FREE

Plus get a FREE surprise gift!

SILHOUETTE® Desire

It's the men you've come
to know and love...
with a bold, new look
that's going to make
you take notice!

MAN of the Month
1994

January: *SECRET AGENT MAN* by Diana Palmer
February: *WILD INNOCENCE* by Ann Major
            (second title in her SOMETHING WILD
            miniseries)
March: *WRANGLER'S LADY* by Jackie Merritt
April: *BEWITCHED* by Jennifer Greene
May: *LUCY and THE STONE* by Dixie Browning
June: *HAVEN'S CALL* by Robin Elliott

And that's just the first six months!
Later in the year, look for books by Barbara Boswell,
Cait London, Joan Hohl, Annette Broadrick and
LassSmall....

MAN OF THE MONTH
ONLY FROM
SIILHOUETTE DESIRE

 **SILHOUETTE®** *Desire*

 **SOMETHING** *Wild*

by Ann Major

Take a walk on the wild side with Ann Major's sizzling
stories featuring Honey, Midnight...and Innocence!

IN SEPTEMBER, YOU EXPERIENCED...

WILD HONEY Man of the Month
A clash of wills set the stage for an electrifying romance for
J. K. Cameron and Honey Wyatt.

NOW ENJOY...

WILD MIDNIGHT November 1993
Heat Up Your Winter
A bittersweet reunion turns into a once-in-a-lifetime adventure for
Lacy Douglas and Johnny Midnight.

AND IN FEBRUARY 1994, LOOK FOR...

WILD INNOCENCE Man of the Month
One man's return sets off a startling chain of events for
Innocence Lescuer and Raven Wyatt.

Let your wilder side take over with this exciting series—only from
Silhouette Desire!

If you missed the first book of SOMETHING WILD, *Wild Honey* (SD #805), order your
copy now by sending your name, address, zip or postal code, along with a check or
money order (please do not send cash) for $2.99 plus 75¢ postage and handling
($1.00 in Canada), payable to Silhouette Books, to:

In the U.S.

3010 Walden Ave.
P. O. Box 9077
Buffalo, NY 14269-9077

In Canada

P. O. Box 636
Fort Erie, Ontario
L2A 5X3

Please specify book title with your order.
Canadian residents add applicable federal and provincial taxes.

SDSW2

SILHOUETTE.... Where Passion Lives

Don't miss these Silhouette favorites by some of our most popular authors!
And now, you can receive a discount by ordering two or more titles!

Silhouette Desire®

#05751	THE MAN WITH THE MIDNIGHT EYES BJ James	$2.89	☐
#05763	THE COWBOY Cait London	$2.89	☐
#05774	TENNESSEE WALTZ Jackie Merritt	$2.89	☐
#05779	THE RANCHER AND THE RUNAWAY BRIDE Joan Johnston	$2.89	☐

Silhouette Intimate Moments®

#07417	WOLF AND THE ANGEL Kathleen Creighton	$3.29	☐
#07480	DIAMOND WILLOW Kathleen Eagle	$3.39	☐
#07486	MEMORIES OF LAURA Marilyn Pappano	$3.39	☐
#07493	QUINN EISLEY'S WAR Patricia Gardner Evans	$3.39	☐

Silhouette Shadows®

#27003	STRANGER IN THE MIST Lee Karr	$3.50	☐
#27007	FLASHBACK Terri Herrington	$3.50	☐
#27009	BREAK THE NIGHT Anne Stuart	$3.50	☐
#27012	DARK ENCHANTMENT Jane Toombs	$3.50	☐

Silhouette Special Edition®

#09754	THERE AND NOW Linda Lael Miller	$3.39	☐
#09770	FATHER: UNKNOWN Andrea Edwards	$3.39	☐
#09791	THE CAT THAT LIVED ON PARK AVENUE Tracy Sinclair	$3.39	☐
#09811	HE'S THE RICH BOY Lisa Jackson	$3.39	☐

Silhouette Romance®

#08893	LETTERS FROM HOME Toni Collins	$2.69	☐
#08915	NEW YEAR'S BABY Stella Bagwell	$2.69	☐
#08927	THE PURSUIT OF HAPPINESS Anne Peters	$2.69	☐
#08952	INSTANT FATHER Lucy Gordon	$2.75	☐

AMOUNT	$	_____
DEDUCT: **10% DISCOUNT FOR 2+ BOOKS**	$	_____
POSTAGE & HANDLING	$	_____
($1.00 for one book, 50¢ for each additional)		
APPLICABLE TAXES*	$	_____
TOTAL PAYABLE	$	_____
(check or money order—please do not send cash)		

To order, complete this form and send it, along with a check or money order for the total above, payable to Silhouette Books, to: *In the U.S.*: 3010 Walden Avenue, P.O. Box 9077, Buffalo, NY 14269-9077; *In Canada*: P.O. Box 636, Fort Erie, Ontario, L2A 5X3.

Name: _____

Address: _____ City: _____

State/Prov.: _____ Zip/Postal Code: _____

*New York residents remit applicable sales taxes.
Canadian residents remit applicable GST and provincial taxes.

SBACK-OD

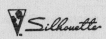